CAELIUS

Elemental's MC
(book 9)

ALEXI FERREIRA

CAELIUS

Elementals MC (Book 9)

Copyright © 2019 Alexi Ferreira

All rights reserved.

This book is a work of fiction and any resemblance to any person or persons, living or dead, any event, occurrence, or incident is purely coincidental. The characters and story lines are created and thought up from the author's imagination or are used fictitiously.

https://alexiferreirawrite.wixsite.com/mysite

Amazon.com/author/alexiferreira

Facebook.com/alexiferreira.writer

To love is risky, not to love is foolish.

Maxime Lagace

Contents

ALEXI FERREIRA

ACKNOWLEDGMENTS

Thank you to my children that believe in me and to my readers for all their support without all of you this dream wouldn't be possible.

ALAIA 1

"How long will it take?" Sara whispers, her blue eyes wide with fear. We have been locked up in this basement for the past two days with minimal contact with anyone, and Joshua promised that no one would find us and that he would come back as soon as it was safe to let us out.

"I don't know, but they're still looking for us," I reply. I felt a disturbance in the earth above us, and I know those evil men are still out there, waiting to grab us. I wish I knew how they found out about us. We have always been so secretive about what we can do; only my family knows about it. Since the day we were born, my parents said they knew we were different. That things felt different when we were around.

"Can you tell if Joshua is okay?" I ask, as my twin can tell how people close to us are doing and where they are. She closes her eyes, a frown appearing between her eyebrows. A minute later, she opens them and looks back at me. Her green eyes so similar to mine are soft with love for our older brother. Joshua always took it into his hands to protect us from the world. When our parents died in a crash three years ago, he took us to live with him.

Joshua got us out of his apartment just in time, two days before there was a break-in. We were all suspicious, as nothing was taken except for some of my and Sara's clothing. As Special Forces, Joshua was naturally on his guard. He noticed the bikers hanging around and paying extra attention to our apartment windows.

Before the break-in, I could feel an evil vibration in the soil in our garden. I have a special gift of being able to make things grow; plants and trees flourish around me like with no one else. Also, when animals are around me, their young are born healthy and flourish. Therefore, when something disturbs the earth, I can feel the different vibrations.

"I wonder if Joshua has found out anything about them," Sara says as she walks towards the pile of blankets we have on the floor and sits down. There isn't much here, as we didn't have much time to prepare. The only things we have are the blankets we have on the floor, which we share when sleeping, and the bag of tinned food we grabbed on the way here.

We were lucky that Joshua knew about this abandoned house and that it had a basement for us to hide in. I don't know how they managed to track us, but they have been close, as I have felt the change in the ground around us. We have no way of contacting Joshua. He took our phones, saying that it was safer not to have anything they might be able to track us by.

"I don't know, but he will have to come soon or we're going to run out of water and food," I say as I look at the two tins of beans and the half loaf of bread we have left.

"Maybe we should just take a chance and leave. We can phone Joshua as soon as we find a place to hide and let him know where we went," Sara says as she pulls a blanket around herself.

"I don't know, Sara. Josh will be furious. Besides, where will we go?" I will gladly leave this place, but to where? We don't want to get anyone involved with whatever this is. Why are these men after us so desperately?

"What about Chrissie's Cabin? You did say that she offered for us to use it anytime we want to." I had thought about it, but I don't know if we should take the risk of moving away from here after Joshua insisted on us staying until he came back for us. Also, how are we going to get there? This cabin is in the middle of nowhere. We will need a car to get there, and we don't have any money.

"We have no way of getting there. What if we come across those men again?" I argue, knowing that Sara is impulsive and will simply head out without a plan, hoping for the best.

"Alaia, stop being so cautious. We will hitchhike. I know it's dangerous, but I believe that sooner or later, they are going to find us here. I know it and you know it." I know they have been closing in, and as Sara says, they're going to figure out we are hiding in here. Somehow, they have pinpointed our location to this area, and I think it will be just a matter of time before they figure out our hiding place.

"We can't go now; I can still feel their evilness." The pain that radiates through the ground up the soles of my feet is disturbing. I know that if we get caught by these men, it will be the end of us, because it isn't possible that evil like this has any compassion.

"Does that mean you're considering the option of us leaving?" Sara asks as she pulls the blanket tighter around her.

"Yes, I'm considering it," I state as I walk towards the wall and place my hands on it. As we are underground, the earth surrounds us, which allows me to feel movement above us easier. I close my eyes and feel the peace that usually surrounds me when I am one with the earth. I don't feel that repressing evilness, but I feel a different type of energy that calls to me. Concentrating on the source of that energy, I focus to try to identify where it's coming from, but the pain, the sorrow that surrounds this energy, has my heart tightening in pain.

There is a magnetism to this energy that has me wanting to hold whoever it is close to me until the pain is alleviated. Something about this energy calls to me, something that has me breathless. I suddenly realize what I'm doing, and I pull my hands away from the wall and look at it curiously. I don't know what is happening. First, I feel an evil energy I have never felt before, and now this.

"What's wrong, Alaia?" Sara asks with a frown when she sees my perplexed look.

"I'm not sure, but I don't feel the evil like I did before."

"Well, let's go, then. We should move before they come back for us." Sara stands hurriedly and starts to make her way towards me, a smile lighting up her face as she looks at me. Go figure, we have men after us, and she's excited for an adventure.

"We need to be careful, Sara. Don't go out there acting irresponsible," I caution as she prepares herself to leave. I collect my jacket in case the temperature changes, and hurry after her to the door. She opens the door and stops, listening for any noise upstairs. After a moment, we quietly make our way upstairs.

When I reach what once was a kitchen but now is four walls with a broken-down cupboard, I stop. "Are we sure we want to do this?" I ask, looking at Sara, who is now standing by the outside door.

She looks over her shoulder at me and frowns. "Don't do this now, Alaia. We agreed that we were going to do this." At her words, I take in a deep breath and nod. I know she's right. If we sit here, we will be in more trouble than if we're moving. We will just have to find a way of letting Joshua know where we are. She opens the door and steps outside. I follow, looking up and down the deserted road. This house is one of many abandoned houses, and we don't want to meet the owners of the ones still occupied, as this is a really rough area.

We hurry down the road with our hoodies covering our heads. When we turn down a side street, we see three bikes riding past a stop sign. My heart starts to race, as I remember the other men riding bikes, but these continue riding. I notice one looking towards us, but they ride past.

"Was that them?" Sara asks as she looks at me.

"I don't think so. I saw the symbol on the back of their jackets, and it didn't look like the other guys' ones," I say, but I hurry across the road they were riding so I don't encounter them in case they decided to turn back.

We are about a block down the road when we hear the noise of motorbikes coming up behind us. "Alaia?" Sara asks as she continues walking without looking back. I know she's asking me if it's the guys hunting us, but without connecting with the ground, I won't be able to tell. I'm also not stopping right now and acting suspicious by placing my hands on the ground or on a tree.

"I can't tell." The roar of the bikes is nearing, and my heart starts to race, but instead of a feeling of fear filling me, that same feeling of nurturing fills my soul. Is it possible that one of these men or all of them is the source from where that feeling is coming from? The bikes start to slow, and my breathing becomes laboured as the feeling increases.

The three bikes slow to a crawl next to us. I look over and see the three men we saw riding down the road earlier. "Hello, ladies." At the greeting, I look toward the bikes Three huge men are sitting comfortably on their bikes, their similar black jackets confirming that they also belong to some kind of club. The guy who spoke has the naughtiest smile I've ever seen in a man, his twinkling eyes proof that his soul isn't as black as the energy I've been feeling the last few days.

"Hi." At my greeting, the guy sitting on his bike just behind him tenses, his head snapping around to look at me. His captivating dark-blue eyes stare at me with an intensity that I can feel right down to my soul. The feeling of nurturing I was feeling earlier overwhelms me now, and all I want to do is walk up to this man and hug him close to me.

"What are two beautiful women like the two of you doing out here? Don't you know this is a neighbourhood you should keep away from?" the same one asks as he switches off his bike and kicks out the stand.

"What is it to you?" Sara asks as she places her hands on her hips.

"Feisty," the one furthest away says, but I don't pay him any attention, as my eyes are still captured in the magnetic stare of the one who has now also switched off his bike and has crossed his arms over the tank of his matte-black bike.

"What's your name?" the one staring at me asks. His soft gravelly voice flows over my body like a ripple over water. Goosebumps raise over me as I see his eyes travel the length of my body as if he can see the affect he is having on me.

"Alaia," I murmur, and notice the quiet that descends at the mention of my name. I see the one who greeted us look back at the one who asked me for my name. I feel like there is some kind of communication that has just passed between these two men that I missed.

"That's a rare name. I haven't heard it before," the one further away says. "Have you heard that name before, Ceric?"

The one who greeted us shakes his head. "Nope, I think it's pretty rare. Have you heard it before, Caelius?" Why does it feel like they are communicating with each other without me knowing what they are actually saying? His name is Caelius. What an interesting name.

"Alaia," Caelius says in his gravelly voice that has me stepping closer to him. I feel a hand on my arm, and only then do I remember Sara is standing next to me. What is wrong with me? How does this man's energy affect me the way it does?

"What are you doing?" Sara asks with a raised brow. Suddenly, I feel a tingling feeling move up my legs. I gasp in surprise, as I have never felt the earth without touching it with my skin, but it seems like I can feel the evil of the other men approaching.

"They're coming," I whisper as I look around. I feel Sara tense, a frightened look on her face.

"Who's coming?" Caelius asks. That low voice of his is tinged with danger.

"We have to go," Sara says as we start to hurry away down the road. I can feel the evil oppressive energy approaching, eating all the goodness of the earth.

"Alaia!" Caelius snaps. "Who's coming?"

"Sorry, we have to go. They're after us," I mutter as I continue hurrying away.

"Stop, we will help you. Come with us, and we will leave now." At his words, I stop, the evil starting to intensify.

"What are you doing, Alaia? We have to hurry," Sara says as she pulls at my arm.

"They can help us, Sara. Think about it. We need a fast way out."

Sara stops and then nods as she makes her way back to the three men. "Okay, if you're going to help us, we need it now and quickly," she says as she walks up to the guy who called her feisty. "I'm Sara." She climbs onto the back of his bike. I see a grin light up his face, and then he starts his bike.

"I'm Gunner," he says. I make my way back to the men and look between the two who are left. I make my way towards Caelius but am stopped at Ceric's words.

"You will come with me." I turn to walk to him and hear Caelius growl, a deep angry noise that courses through my body. Ceric puts his hands up, a frown marring his face. "You know this is better, Brother." I look over my shoulder at Caelius and then tense. A murderous look is on his face as he stares at Ceric. What is going on here? Why is he so angry?

"We really need to go," Sara calls as she looks behind her. I raise my eyes and see five men hurrying towards us by foot.

I turn and hurry towards Caelius's bike. "Come on already. We don't have time for this," I say urgently as I sit on his bike. He looks over his shoulder and then moves towards his bike with a speed that has me gasping in surprise. I feel him pull my arms around his waist as he leans forwards over the tank of the bike, and we speed down the road and away from the evilness starting to infiltrate every grain of soil around us.

CAELIUS 2

The minute I heard her voice, my body came alive. A feeling I haven't felt in a very long time overwhelmed me. I have been filled with a feeling of helplessness for so long that being once again filled with purpose has me at odds with things around me. When I finally had my woman in front of me, my heart was beating so hard that I couldn't even hear myself think. All I could think about was that my salvation was before me.

When a little while back I found her photo and realized she was my woman, I had already lost all hope. I thought there was nothing more for me to do on this earth, that my brothers would be fine, as most of them had found their women, that I could now end my miserable life. Now, she explodes into my life with everything I had already given up on.

When Ceric proposed to take Alaia with him, my anger rose with such speed that it surprised me. Since what happened to me, I have kept all my emotions bottled up. If I hadn't, I would have turned berserker and gone on a killing spree to appease the rage that consumed me. I am always the voice of reason because I don't let my emotions take the better of me. Therefore, when I reacted the way I did, Ceric was shocked—not only him, but I was too.

I shouldn't have let my emotions take over as I did. After so long, I was overwhelmed by emotions, and now I have touched Alaia. Our bonding has begun, and she doesn't even know who we are or who I am to her. Many years ago, when I still let myself imagine how it would be with my mate, I never for once thought I would start our bonding like this. I always thought I would explain everything to her first, give her a chance to get to know me.

Well, now it's too late. Alaia is going to be mine, and there is nothing or no one that can change that. When I saw the fear in her eyes, I wanted to go on a rampage. I know she's scared of the Keres, as I felt their foul presence just before we left. If they did anything to her like they did to some of our other women, I'm going to go out and find every one of them and skin them.

Her arms around my body have me hard as a rock. Her breasts rubbing against my back make me want to stop the bike and make her mine. We have just turned into the compound grounds when I feel her start to convulse behind me. My heart races as I stop the bike. To not unseat her, I continue holding her arms around me as I pull one of my legs over the bike and stand. Loosening her arms, I continue holding them as I turn around. When I can finally pick her up off the bike, I hold her close to my chest. Bringing my wrist up to my mouth, I tear at it with my teeth and place it over her mouth.

"Open your mouth, Alaia," I say quietly as I hear the other two bikes approaching. I turn my back to them, as this is something private between my mate and me, and I will not share it with anyone else. I hear Sara start to complain as Gunner continues up the path. I know Ceric will stay behind to protect my back, but he knows better than to approach.

I see the blood trickle into my woman's mouth, and I smile, a real smile, something I haven't done in a very long time. When she starts to quieten, I pull my wrist away and cuddle her closer to me. Looking over my shoulder, I see Ceric standing next to his bike with his back to us as he keeps an eye on our surroundings.

"I'm going to take her up to the compound."

Ceric turns at my statement and grins. "Welcome to the club, Brother. Prepare yourself, because you are so fucked now." He wiggles his brows jokingly, which has me shaking my head in exasperation, but I can feel my lips pulling into a smile.

"She's nothing like your woman," I state, and Ceric's grin grows wider. Nova is a good woman, but she's always getting herself and the other women into trouble with her ideas.

"Of course not. No one is like my hellcat," he quips as he shrugs. "But don't worry, she'll give you grief in her own way." With those words, I start to make my way up the path that will lead to the compound. "Hey, Caelius." I stop and turn around. "Congratulations, Brother. You deserve to have found your woman."

I know my brothers have been worried about me, and they would have been so much more worried if they knew how close I have come to ending my life. After everything that was done to me, I lost the will to continue, but my brothers kept me here, the responsibility of keeping them safe holding me by their side. But when they started to find their mates, that responsibility started to lighten. Now that I have found my mate, I feel the constant melancholy lifting.

I am pleased with my mate, her lustrous long strawberry-blonde locks hanging over my arm. Her beautiful light-green eyes now closed had a tendency to shine with an internal light that had me hypnotized. The way she was looking at me with such tenderness had my stomach clutching in knots.

"I will always be by your side." I know she can't hear me, but I need to say it. I have been closed to everyone around me, only talking when necessary. I know my brothers were always there for me, but I couldn't unburden myself on them. Draco has tried to open me up to life again, tried to find out what happened when I was held by those freaks, but I've been a coward and have never been able to open up to anyone.

Years ago, when I was captured, I know my brothers looked for me day and night, but it took weeks before I was free, and in those weeks, that group of vampire hunters, as they called themselves, had a chance to prod me in every way possible. I know Draco blames himself for not getting to me earlier, but I don't blame any of them. I would rather it be me they did those things to than any other of my brothers.

I thought a part of me was dead, but now with this woman in my arms, I feel alive again. I feel like my old self, something I never thought I would feel again. I walk into the bar area and come face to face with Sara, with Gunner standing behind her. When he sees me, he lifts his hands in the air in exasperation. "What's wrong with her? Alaia, sweetie, what's wrong?" Sara asks worriedly.

"She's fine. She just needs to rest," I say as I continue making my way to my room, but she places her hand on my arm to stop me, which has my skin crawling in irritation at another woman touching me. The men didn't exaggerate; we really do have an aversion to all other women except our mates. I grunt in irritation, which has Gunner stepping in and pulling her away.

"Let Caelius take your sister to rest. Don't worry, you will be able to see her as soon as she's feeling better," Gunner says persuasively. "Besides, we have a medic who will have a look at her, but you must let Caelius go." Sara reluctantly lets go of my arm. I can see she's suspicious, but her concern for her sister wins, and she hesitantly steps back. I continue making my way down the corridor towards my room; I can feel the possessiveness, the protectiveness, that I feel for this woman, and I don't know what to do with it. My emotions have been repressed for so long that I don't know what to do with all these feelings and thoughts bombarding me.

As I approach my room, I see Wulf and Draco walking towards me, concerned looks on their faces. "Caelius, who is she?" Draco asks as he looks at Alaia against my chest, and then his head snaps up at me. "Is she your woman?"

"Yes," I grunt as I continue on my way to my room. I know that Wulf and Draco won't say anything else, as they know how volatile we get when first bonding.

Walking in, I kick the door closed after me and stand for a few minutes, looking around. I wonder if my woman is going to like her new home. I haven't done much with my room because I didn't expect to find my mate. I know it's sparse, but if Alaia wants to change anything, she can.

I look at everything with a critical eye and shrug. The only things in the room are a king-sized bed, a floor-to-ceiling mirror, and a desk with a chair. There are two doors to the side. One leads to a walk-in closet, and the other one to the bathroom. I gently lay her on the middle of the bed and then stand up to look down at her.

My erection is straining against the zipper of my jeans as I look at her petite figure. Her upper body is covered with her hoodie, but I can tell she's got luscious breasts. Her lower body is encased in tight black jeans, and her hands are lying next to her body. I lift one of mine and look at it critically and then turn back to hers. She is tiny compared to me. I'm going to have to be extra careful with this woman of mine to never hurt her.

When she awakens, I'm going to have to explain everything to her and hope that she doesn't run out of here screaming. What will I do if she doesn't want to complete our bond? Can I let her go? Can I put both of us through that hell? If we don't bond, there will be an emptiness within us that nothing can fill except each other. I walk towards the closet. Opening the door, I step in and pull out a black T-shirt from the pile of other black T-shirts here. I take hold of the bottom of the one I'm wearing and pull it over my head, my eyes as always going to the mirror on the opposite wall.

The scars running up my back and down my arms and chest are visible under my tattoos. Elementals don't scar except when they are not allowed to heal time and time again. Salt and other acids were placed in my wounds as experiments. When I was first found, it took Bion weeks to get me healed, and even like that, the scars never left me. Not only the scars on the outside but the ones on the inside too.

I wonder what Alaia will think of me when she sees my body. Will she be repulsed like I am? I wasn't thinking. I should never have let her touch me. I should have given her the opportunity to choose, to see what I am, but I've taken that choice away, and now we will have to bond. I hear a moaning sound, and I snap around to see her eyes on me.

"What happened?" she mumbles, her eyes wide with horror, her hand against her chest. Fuck, I should have been paying attention. I hurriedly place the T-shirt over my head and down my torso.

"You passed out," I say, and am about to start explaining everything, when she starts to shake her head and point at me.

"No, what happened to your back?" I can feel the knot in my stomach when I realize what she is asking. My throat feels like sandpaper when I think of what she saw, the horror on her face testament to what she thinks of my scars. I know I have to tell her sooner or later about what happened, as that is what has moulded me into the man I am today, but I wasn't expecting to do it now.

"I was held by vampire hunters. They tortured me for several weeks before I was able to get away." Shit, I should maybe have rephrased that. She snaps to her knees and stretches out her hand until she's holding mine. The feel of her warm hand against mine has me tightening all over, warmth filtering through my body, touching me in a way that has me calming. I see tears in her eyes as she looks up at me. My heart tightens at the sight of her tears, and I want to kill someone.

"Don't cry." My voice is gruff. I feel a knot in my throat at the sight of her distress.

"How could people do that? The pain you must have felt. The pain you still feel." At her words, I feel my entire body tense. Does she somehow know the thoughts that had crossed my mind before meeting her? It's one thing to want to put an end to myself before the fury in me took over, but it's another to have your mate thinking you are weak, that you are suicidal.

"What do you mean?" I regret my snapped question the minute it's out.

Her eyes widen, and she pulls her hand away. "I'm sorry, it's just so awful." She turns her eyes down to the bed as she sits back, clearly lying to me. What does she know that she's not saying?

"Alaia, what aren't you telling me?" At my question, her eyes snap back to mine in surprise. "I know you have some kind of gift. All the women the Keres are after do."

She gasps and sits straighter as her hands start to twist with nerves. "Is that why those men were after us?" I nod, and she pales. "How did they find out?"

"They have equipment that measures your energy levels."

"How would you know that? Do you also do it?"

I can see the worry in her eyes, and I want to enfold her in my arms to calm her fears. "No, but we fight the Keres to try to stop them from kidnapping women like you. You see, all the women here at the compound are like you in some way or another." She frowns, a cute wrinkle appearing between her eyebrows that makes me want to lean down and kiss her forehead.

"There are other women here with special gifts?" At my nod, she moves closer to me. "What gifts have they got?"

I nearly smile at her curiosity; she's just like a kitten. "We have Jasmine who can see into the future, Gabriela who can tell about a person by touching them, Talia who can move stuff with her mind, Brielle is a healer, Scarlett can sense the truth, Aria can hear a person's thoughts, Nova has the gift of persuasion, and Saskia can feel energies. What about you, kitten? What can you do?" I can see her surprised look at the revelation of the women's gifts.

"They can really do all that?"

"Yes, they can. You will meet them and see for yourself." She claps her hands and hurriedly stands from the bed and then sways, which has me picking her up and holding her against my chest before she has a chance to fall. She gasps in surprise as her hand moves over my chest to my neck and her head leans back so she's looking up at me. Looking down at her beautiful eyes, I can't resist, and lower my head, my lips touching hers. Her sweetness is like nectar, her essence surrounding me in a peace I haven't felt in a very long time.

I feel her soft fingers entwine in my hair, and her lips part, letting me take possession. My cock is as hard as steel fighting against the tightness of my jeans. Soon I will lose all control; I can feel my control slipping with each stroke of our tongues. I pull back and see her eyes opening, a dazed look to them, which has me wanting to lower my head again.

"Wow . . . you can kiss," she mutters. I smile at her surprise. I know she's feeling the connection between us. Even though we haven't bonded yet, the connection is there and it's strong. The pull is undeniable. Our hearts are already beating at the same pace. Lowering myself to the bed with her on my lap, I groan when I realize my mistake as her ass moves over my erection. Fuck, I can't concentrate on this conversation if she keeps moving around.

"Alaia," I grunt as she once again moves. My hands clutch her waist and hold her still. "I need to tell you something."

"Mmm," she murmurs as she looks at me, passion still clearly stamped on her face.

"You're mine."

At my growled words, her head snaps back and she frowns.

ALAIA 3

"Wha . . . what?" Did I hear him right? I'm sure he said I'm his; his kiss must have messed with my mind. I can still feel the blood roaring through my veins. This man before me can kiss like no one else has ever kissed me before.

"I'm an Elemental. All the brothers here including myself have gifts like you."

He's like me? I've never met anyone like me or my sister before. Now in one day, I get to know a whole lot of people who are different like us. "Is this like a special gifts colony or something?"

He throws back his head and roars with laughter. He doesn't laugh for long, as he seems surprised to be laughing, but there is definitely a twinkle in his eyes. "Or something," he says. "We're the Elementals MC, a motorbike club. As Elementals, we can each bend a specific element."

My curiosity rises. Wow, if this is true, it must be so awesome to be able to bend the elements. "What can you do?"

"I bend air."

I look around, looking for something I can ask him to move. "Can you lift that T-shirt that you dropped in your wardrobe with your gift?" At my question, his eyebrow rises. "Or if not, maybe a piece of paper?" I wonder where I can get a piece of paper; I look around but don't find anything that could hold paper. Is this his room? It is really bare.

I feel a breeze on my cheek. My eyes snap to his, and I see him rotating his hands in an anti-clockwise motion. Is he going to try lifting the T-shirt? And then I feel myself lifting off him. Looking down, I realize he's lifting me with air. Wow, to say I'm surprised is an understatement. I hold out my arms and let the wind lift me until I'm about two feet above his lap. I can feel the grin stretching across my face. This is so cool.

"You have such a great gift." At my words, he shakes his head in amusement, and then I'm being lowered gently onto his lap again. I feel myself blushing as his hardness slides just right against my jeans. Both of us groan, which has my cheeks darkening with colour.

"What gift do you have?" he asks.

I hesitate, as I have never willingly revealed what Sara and I can do, but seeing as he opened up to me, it's only right that I share our secret with him.

"I can make things grow, like plants or sick animals." At my words, he smiles and nods. "Sara can find anyone close to her and see where they are and what they are doing at any specific time."

"Your sister also has a gift?" His surprised tone makes me smile. I guess it isn't every day they find people with gifts, especially sisters.

"Yes, she does." I wonder if he will be able to tell Sara and me apart. Sometimes people have difficulty telling who we are. For the first time in my life, I don't want someone to get me confused with her. Caelius with his imposing presence has me trembling as his strong hand strokes my hip, the other gently holding my leg.

"How did you manage to get away from the Keres?" I notice his tone has lowered, and there is an intense look in his beautiful blue eyes that has chills rising up my back. His fingers on my leg tighten. I can clearly see the hate on his face and wonder how deep and what kind of bad blood flows between the Elementals and the Keres.

"My brother Joshua helped us escape when we noticed that there were men following us and keeping track of all our movements."

"Why didn't you go to the police?"

"Joshua was in the marines, and he reckoned that by the time the cops did anything, those men would have already done what they wanted with us." He nods as he continues looking at me, waiting for me to finish. "He took us to an abandoned house that he knew of, but somehow they found our location. They hadn't pinpointed it yet, but they were close, so Sara and I decided to leave before they did, and let Joshua know once we were safe."

"You can contact your brother later, let him know you are safe and that no Keres will get close to you again."

I begin to relax. Unconsciously, I was worried that this was all a ploy to try to get Sara and me to accompany them to their home, but at his words, I feel peace again. As my eyes encounter his deep examination, a chill races up my spine. I don't know what this man has, but I feel so comfortable with him. I feel as if I've known him for years; meanwhile, it's only been a couple hours, and what am I doing on his bed and sitting on him like this?

I have never felt like this before. It's a pull, like I need to be touching him constantly. I can feel his pain, pain that I now know has something to do with what happened to him. My nurturing nature is screaming that I hold him close until the pain is washed away and his inner child nourishes and once again frolics with joy.

"What did you mean I'm yours?" I can feel him tensing underneath me, his muscular arms bulging. I don't know what I want his answer to be. I'm confused by how much this man attracts me. I lower my eyes from his to his lips. They are slightly parted, and his perfect white teeth are just visible. I want to lean forward and kiss him, kiss him until I can't think any longer, kiss him until this attraction I'm feeling fades.

"As an Elemental, I will only ever be able to bond with one woman. You, Alaia, are my woman." I hear his words, but my body seems to be having a mind of its own. I know he must be saying this just to get me into bed, but at the moment, I don't care, because I have never wanted to be with someone as much as I want Caelius.

"Are you going to kiss me sometime today?" Did I just say that? I can feel my cheeks warming as I realize what I just blurted out. I don't have time to think of anything else, because suddenly, he pulls me against his chest and his lips crash down on mine. The warmth of his lips is like lava that burns through my body in the most erotic manner. My ears are ringing as I hear the blood rushing through my veins. His one hand is on my hip, holding my hips still when all I want is to rub myself up and down on the hardness I feel between my legs. His other hand is coiled in my hair as he holds my head still while he kisses me. One minute, I'm straddling him. The other, I'm lying on the bed and he's leaning over me as his lips trail down my neck. My heart is racing as I feel his hard body against the softness of mine.

"You are so beautiful," he mutters against my skin, the hand that was behind my head now moving down over my ribs until it reaches the edge of my hoodie. Here it stops as he lifts his head and looks deep into my eyes.

"Don't stop," I urge.

"Alaia, are you sure?" His voice is deep, nearly a growl, his eyes intense as if boring into my soul. I should stop. I should at least think about it, but what the hell? I only live once, and at the moment, the hottest guy I have ever met is waiting for me to say yes so he can make passionate love to me. There is no way I'm going to tell him to stop. Instead, I raise my hand and pull his head back down so he can continue kissing my neck.

I smile when I hear him groan, and then his hand is under my hoodie and he's stroking his thumb over my erect nipple. It's me who groans then in pleasure, his thumb and index finger pinching the nipple gently until a burning pleasure is coursing from my nipple down to the moistness between my legs. He stops kissing me once again as he sits up and, with both hands, pulls my hoodie up and over my head. My cheeks are hot with embarrassment as he looks over my chest. I see his tongue flicker out and moisten his lips, which has me whimpering, as I want those lips all over me.

His hands cup my breasts and squeeze gently before he unclasps my bra, and it falls open, revealing my naked breasts to him. "I'm going to make you mine." With those words, he leans and kisses first one nipple and then the other before he starts to suckle and nip at my nipple. A pleasure like I have never felt before fills me. I lift my hips so that I can feel his body against mine. Moving in a rhythm older than time, I rub against him, winning a deep growl out of him as he bites down harder on my breast.

"Oh, yes," I mutter as an emptiness fills me. I need more, so much more. One of his hands is at the waistband of my jeans as he pulls down the zip and opens them. He roughly pulls the jeans down until they are around my thighs. His hand wanders to the heat radiating from my body, and he cups me, moving his hand in a rubbing motion that has me squirming in pleasure.

I place my hand on his chest that is still covered with a T-shirt and feel his muscles rippling under my fingers. I saw the scars on his body when he was changing, but that did not detract from the beauty of his body. He is sculptured like a god. His tattoos, the little I was able to see before he hid himself with his T-shirt again, spoke of pain. I run my fingers down until I feel skin and realize that I have bunched the T-shirt up and am now touching his firm abdomen. My mind is a pool of passion as I feel his finger enter my heat as his thumb strokes my wanting clit.

"Caelius." I gasp as I feel the pleasure building in my depths. He inserts another of his fingers, and he moves them to a rhythm that is driving me crazy. I move my hand down over the bulge in his jeans and rub, feeling the dampness of them that professes to how horny he is. "Take your clothes off," I mutter, as I want to feel him plunge into my depths, but he ignores my plea as he continues to play with my body. I feel my insides tense and know that I won't be able to hold back any longer.

"Cae . . . lius." I gasp as I convulse with my orgasm, my whole body vibrating with its release. Before I can recuperate or even think, I feel Caelius move away from me. Then my jeans are being pulled down my legs and off, together with my sneakers. I want to complain and hold him back, but my body is too relaxed to build up the energy needed for it. I hear rustling but don't open my eyes until I feel Caelius return to my side and feel his skin against mine. My eyes shoot open, and I see him in all his naked glory above me.

"Are you sure, Alaia?" I can hear the hesitation in his voice, and my heart once again goes out to the pain I can see in his eyes. I lift my hand and place it flat over a tattoo that covers a jagged scar on his side.

"Yes, I'm sure." Even if I had doubt, I would never stop at a time like this, and besides, it's not as if I'm not having the best pleasure of my life. He doesn't say anything else as he grabs my hips with both hands and pulls me closer to him, and then he lowers his head and kisses my lower stomach before he moves down and slides his tongue over my clit in a gentle motion that has my hand holding his head closer to me. He has me gasping and squirming in no time at all. When I start feeling like I won't be able to hold on much longer, he sits back and takes his enlarged cock in one of his hands and rubs it over my lower lips, my wetness coating his maleness until he slides slowly into my body. I can feel my muscles stretching to accommodate his girth, but the sensation of fullness is so good that I lift my bum and feel him deepen even more.

He pulls out slightly and then plunges. I gasp, not in pain but with the feeling of perfection once we are both joined fully. He waits a few seconds before he pulls out partially and then starts to move with a motion like the waves in a destressed ocean. The feeling of being one overwhelms me, his corded muscles professing to his strength as he pleasures both of us. He leans down on his elbows and takes my lips in a blistering kiss that has me tightening around him. I want this feeling to last forever, but I know I won't be able to hold on.

"I'm going to bond both of us. For that, we need to share blood." At his words, I frown. Did he say blood? But then my thoughts scatter as my orgasm explodes, leaving me gasping as I feel something warm dribbling over my lips into my mouth. "I join us forever and always. Where one goes, the other shall follow. I will hold you above everyone and everything else. I will protect you until my last breath. My body, soul, and mind are forever yours, and yours are mine." I feel tears fill my eyes at the beautiful words. They seem nearly like a vow, but then I feel a sharp pain as Caelius bites the side of my breast, and I lose all sense of time as my body convulses again with such power that I swear I don't hear anything around me except for the beating of our hearts.

I don't know how long we lay here, but I become aware of Caelius's arms around me as my head rests on his chest. I can hear his heart beating under my ear, his unique essence engulfing me. Our naked bodies entwined feel right. How did this happen so quickly? One minute I'm running away; the next, I'm having the best sex of my life. My body is still vibrating with the ecstasy that I felt, but it's not just the sex. There is a feeling of nurturing that I have never felt before, a feeling of rightness that I only ever feel when I'm connected to nature. This man completes me like only nature has ever done before.

"Are you okay?" I hear the gruffness in his voice; this man is so darn sexy. I wish I had met him under better circumstances. He says we will be safe here, and I believe him, but what will happen when the threat is gone? Will he even want to see me again, or is this a one-time thing?

"I'm fine. That was mind-blowing. I hope you don't expect me to leave right away, as I don't think my legs are capable yet." I try to joke, but my heart is squeezing at the thought of never feeling his arms around me again. I feel him tensing under me, and his arms tighten around me, bringing me closer to him.

"You're not going anywhere." His gruff reply has the vice around my heart loosening slightly.

"Would be nice to be here the whole day, but Sara must be worried about me." I know Sara can see how I'm doing, and she'll be fine, so I don't know why I'm giving excuses when all I want to do is stay here.

"Alaia, you are not going anywhere. We are now bonded; you are mine like I am yours. I told you." I pull away slightly so I can look up at his face. His eyes are closed, but his features are tense. I lift my hand and gently stroke his cheek. I know what I'm hearing, but I do not understand. How can he expect me to be his, as he says, just because we slept together?

"What does being yours mean?" He opens his eyes and looks down at me, his dark-blue eyes seeming black at this angle. "It means there is no other woman for me and definitely no other man for you. We are together now, and nothing or no one will change that."

We are dating? When did this happen? "Shouldn't I have a say in this?" Before he can answer, a burning sensation traverses down my side, as if needles are plunging into my skin. I gasp and quickly sit up; Caelius has me off the bed and in his arms before I can even gasp again.

"What's wrong?" There is worry in his eyes as he looks down at me, his eyes traveling over my body and then stopping at my side. When I look down, I see a fiery red mark starting at the top of my hip, up my side to just under my armpit. The burning worsens, and a mark starts to appear. Caelius sits on the edge of the bed and places his hand over the mark. His head lowers, and he kisses my neck tenderly. "It will get better soon." At his words, I frown. How does he know whether it will get better? And why am I in this pain? Did he do something to me?

"What's happening?" I ask, groaning as little pinpricks traverse the length of my side. I feel like the pain is slowly lessening, but it's still burning like a flame is close to my skin.

"It's our bonding mark. Soon, the pain and burning sensation will be gone and my mark will be visible on your skin."

What! Is he crazy?

"What do you mean your mark? Did you give me something? I don't do drugs." I need him to understand that I'm not okay with drugs, and if he somehow gave me something without my knowledge, then I can't be with him.

"Good to know," he grunts as he looks at me, "but I didn't give you anything except to bond with you."

"I don't understand what you mean with that." He keeps saying we're bonded, that I'm his, but how is that possible? I pull his hand away from the area that is still burning but not as intensely, and gasp. There before my eyes is an intricate mark covering my side. I lift my eyes to his and stare.

"What the hell is happening?"

CAELIUS 4

I can see the suspicion on her face, the fear slowly taking root. I want to appease her. Lifting my hand, I move it to her face, but she pushes it away. The thought of her rejecting our bond has a knot growing in my stomach. I cannot let her go now that we're bonded. Not only would it be detrimental to her, but I wouldn't survive without her anymore.

"I told you that we are Elementals. We only have one mate. You, Alaia, are my mate." She shakes her head at my explanation. "I know this is confusing, but I'm sure you can feel the connection we both have with each other." At my words, she nods, but there is still uncertainty on her face.

"When I heard you talk, everything within me knew that you were my other half. When we bond, our hearts beat together." I take her hand and place it on my chest. Her eyes lower to our clasped hands and then lift again to mine. "We are compatible in every way. Once Elementals bond, our connection grows and we become as one. I will need you near me as you will want me near you. We will crave each other's company, and that never diminishes. If anything, it grows with time."

"You are crazy," she says as she shakes her head and tries to move away from me, but I won't let that happen until she understands what it means to be a mate.

"Wait, kitten, let me prove to you what I mean is true."

"How can you explain this?" she argues as she points down at her side. "Does this even go away?"

"No, it doesn't. Your mark is the same as the one I have on my arm. See?" I turn my arm slightly for her to be able to see the top of my shoulder down to my wrist. My birthmark is the replica of the one she now has on her side, except hers is smaller.

"What did you do to me? Am I hallucinating?" At her question, I shake my head in answer. "This isn't possible. A person doesn't just get a mark out of thin air."

"I thought you would realize that there is so much more out there in the world than what people think," I explain urgently. "You have a gift; all the women here have different gifts. We as Elementals move the elements. It's not hard to think that there is something out there that can do this."

"But I don't even know you."

"You know me better than you think; this connection between us is unique between the Elementals. Only mates can feel it." I lower my head and take her lips in a blistering kiss that will leave no doubt in her mind that we are meant to be. At first, she doesn't respond, but then it's as if a floodgate opens, and she returns the kiss with such passion that I am once again at the brink of taking her. Pulling away, I see her dazed look. "I won't push you. I will give you time to get used to me and to everyone around here."

She doesn't answer straightaway as she looks at me intently, but then she slowly nods in acquisition, which has the knot in my stomach loosening slightly. I'm about to talk again, when I hear footsteps approaching my room, and I tense. I want more time with Alaia without interruptions, but I understand that her sister is worried about her. "Your sister is about to knock on the door. Do you want me to tell her to leave or let her in?" By her gasp and her rush off my lap to search for her clothes, I can tell she will have me let her sister in. Just then, there is a hard knock on the door.

"Alaia, I know you're in there. Open up or I'm coming in," Sara says angrily as she bangs on the door again. I lean down and pick up my T-shirt from the ground and then slip it over my head. Looking around, I find my jeans and slip them on as I stand and make my way towards the door. I see Alaia struggling with her jeans, and I wait by the door as she wiggles into them, feeling my hardness twitching in reaction.

She looks over at me, and then I see her face flame in colour at my appreciative look. "Please open the door or she will barge in," she says worriedly as she looks around. I open the door and step back to let a very irritated Sara in. Gunner is standing behind her with his arms crossed over his chest, a frown on his face.

"Sorry, Brother, I held her back as long as I could," he mutters quietly so as not to let the women hear. Sara has hurried into the room and is now standing before Alaia with her hands on her hips.

"Do you know how worried I was?" Sara says.

"We both know that you could see I was fine. What is this about?" Alaia says calmly as she raises her brow at her identical sister, but I will never mistake them, as I will always know my woman even if blinded.

"You were unconscious when you came in, and then when I checked, you were, you know," Sara says as she points to me and then to her sister. "You are not impulsive. This is not like you."

Alaia looks over at me, and I see her eyes travel the length of my body, and then she looks back at her sister. "Have you looked at him?" she whispers to her sister, but unknowingly to them, I can hear her clearly. "You can't tell me you wouldn't be impulsive too." I see Sara look over at me and run her eyes over me too. I raise my brow at them, which has both of them blushing as they quickly look away.

"Yes, he is hot, but what were you thinking? They are supposed to be helping us. What if now he doesn't want anything to do with you? I know you, Alaia. You will be hurt." At her words, I tense as I see my kitten biting her bottom lip. Striding forward, I place my arms around her waist and pull her back against my body.

"Sara, I understand you are worried about your sister, but I want to assure you that I will never hurt her. All I want is to make her happy and to keep her and you safe." Sara looks down at my arms that are around Alaia's waist, and then up to her sister's face, which I can't see. She then looks around to Gunner, who is leaning against the doorframe of the room.

"Can I trust him?" At her words, I look at Gunner and see him nod, which has my curiosity piqued at why she would trust him and why he has taken it onto himself to be her bodyguard. "Okay, then, but know this," Sara says as she looks back at me, "we have a brother who knows all kinds of martial arts and can defend us. If you hurt her in any way, he will make you pay."

"Sara," Alaia gasps in anger.

"It's okay, kitten. Your sister is worried about you." I like the fact that Sara is looking after her sister, and I have a feeling these two are very close.

"Draco wants a meeting," Gunner interrupts, which has the three of us looking over at him as he holds up his phone.

"What, now?" I ask, knowing that it must be important because Draco would not call me in knowing that I have just bonded.

"Yeah, afraid so," he mutters as he stands up straight. I lean down and kiss Alaia gently on the neck before stepping back and getting my boots on.

"Why don't the two of you rest here for as long as you want. As soon as the meeting is over, I will come get you so you can have something to eat," I offer.

"Thank you. That will be great," Alaia says as I turn and make my way towards Gunner. He steps back into the corridor and waits for me to close my bedroom door.

"Are you okay, Brother?" he asks with a frown. Gunner hasn't been with us long compared to the others, as he was human, but because of an accident, he nearly died and, because of that, was changed by mistake. Bion's woman, Brielle, gave him Elemental blood , and that changed him to a superior. He isn't exactly Elemental, as he can't bend the elements, but he is faster, hears better, and is stronger than normal. For a short time, we thought he wouldn't survive the change, but he is strong and made it.

"I'm good."

"How does it feel to be mated? I see the guys with their women, and it's scary to see how much they need the presence of their women. Doesn't it ever worry you that your woman won't want to be your mate?" he asks with a frown.

"Of course it's a worry, as we only have one, but remember, whatever we feel, our mate feels the same. Therefore, it's very rare to have a female who doesn't want to be bonded with an Elemental," I state as we enter the courtyard and see Jasmine and Gabriela sitting on the bench with Orion sitting at their feet, playing on a blanket, and the twins sitting in their pram. That has always been something I have craved but have never told anyone.

To have a mate and children fulfils all my dreams. I will protect Alaia and hopefully any children we may have with my life, and I know that my brothers will always be there too if for some reason I'm not able to protect them.

"Caelius, is it true?" Gabriela calls out, which has Jasmine looking around at us.

"Yes."

"Can we go meet her?" Jasmine asks with a happy smile. I want to smile at her exuberance. All the women at the compound are protected by all of us, not just because we feel we have to because of our code but because they have all become family. They are all caring in their own way and all have a unique and special way about them.

These women are strong and complement their men in every way. I just hope Alaia is half as strong as these women, because some of them have been through hell and are still smiling, always ready to fight for what they believe, like we are.

Elementals are warriors who fight for what we believe is right, and our women are the same. If someone attacks one of us, they attack all of us. I hope Alaia loves being here as much as the other women do, that she can become friends with the others and can find a family here.

"Sure, but her sister is with her," I say as I continue on my way to the computer room.

"Caelius!" I stop and look back at Gabriela in question. "I'm happy for you," she says with a kind smile that has a knot rising in my throat. I nod and follow Gunner until we enter the computer room and find our seats. Everyone is already here and seated and basically just waiting for us.

"What took you so long?" Cassius grumbles as he leans back in his chair.

"Didn't you hear?" Ceric asks with a raised brow. "Our boy here has bonded. Can't you see how bright his energy is, and his new walk." He laughs. "You can see he is lighter; all that pent-up sexual frustration he was hiding has miraculously vanished." I shake my head at Ceric's ploy to tease me as the others grin.

"Okay, now that we're all here, let's start," Draco calls out from the head of the table. I look over at Draco and frown. Something is wrong. Draco is tense, and his eyes are shining like the hounds of hell are loose. "Celmund, update everyone so we are all on the same page."

"I have found Vercin, and you guys won't believe where he is hiding." At his words, I frown. For him to be so animated, it means this must be exciting.

"Do you really want us to guess?" Burkhart says sarcastically as he folds his arms across his chest. Since bonding with Saskia, Burkhart has stayed close to the compound. Before, we were all worried when he used to disappear for days. Saskia has calmed the anger that used to rage inside of him because of the death of his sister. Now he grumbles, but it usually fades away, as that anger that always used to ignite at the slightest provocation is gone.

"No, you would never guess anyway," Celmund quips with a shrug, which has Brandr elbowing Burkhart in amusement. "Vercin is hiding in one of the FBI's safe houses, and the agent in charge is no other than Katya." At his words, I see Wulf tense and look over at Draco, who nods at him. Katya and Wulf had a fling before Wulf met Jasmine. At the time, this was a problem, as Katya insisted on continuing their relationship even though Wulf wanted nothing to do with her, but the women soon sorted Katya out. Nova with her gift of persuasion convinced Katya to leave Wulf alone and never to bother him again.

"Has she always been part of this?" Wulf asks angrily as he looks at Celmund.

"I don't think so. Remember, Aria read her mind and there was nothing," Draco interjects. "We think this is something new."

"When do we go in and kill the fucker?" Cassius asks with a raised brow.

"Yeah, we've had enough of that motherfucker messing with us," Bjarni states as he bangs his hand on the table. Draco nods and then stands as he walks towards where Celmund is and inclines his head for him to sit.

"We're not going to wait for this one. We don't know how long he has been there hiding. Therefore, I want us out of here tonight; I also want the women with us. If we get Vercin today, that is the end of the Keres or until they find another leader, and as you know, that will take time."

"Hell yeah," Bion says with a nod.

"Who's staying?" Ceric asks with a raised brow. Draco looks around at everyone, a pensive look on his face.

"I think we're all going except for Celmund, who needs to keep track of our movements. The women will be helping us, so there will be no bright plans from them. I also have Tor and his men on the way here as we speak. Five of them will patrol the grounds, and the others will join us, as we know there will be double our numbers in Keres there." Draco looks around at everyone and then places his hands on the table as he leans forward. "There will be a war today, a war that we have been expecting and looking forward to for many years. The only difference is that you now have mates and even some children you need to also think about; therefore, if there is anyone here who does not want to join this fight today, I want you to stay behind."

"Fuck no," Bjarni grunts as he stands up.

"I'm fucking killing that son of a bitch," Cassius says as he also stands.

"No, you're not, because I'm reaching him first," Ceric says with a raised brow, standing with the other two.

I stand and simply look at Draco and nod; Wulf, Brandr, and Burkhart stand simultaneously. "I'm fucking going, not staying behind like a wimp," Burkhart grunts as Bion and Gunner also stand. Draco stands up straight and places his fist to his chest.

We all follow by placing our fists to our chests as an oath to the purpose we are about to undergo. We have never in all the years separated. In difficult situations, we pull together. It's not now that we are about to catch Vercin that we are going to separate.

ALAIA 5

Sara is still complaining about how I shouldn't be sleeping with anyone here while we are still running, when I stop listening. I don't want anything to darken the wonderful feeling I am having at the moment. I never thought I could feel like this, and so quickly. I know that everything Caelius said sounds crazy, but how did I get a tattoo out of the blue? I thought of telling Sara and showing her the mark, but I know she would freak and insist on leaving here.

In all good conscience, I wouldn't be able to let her go by herself, and I know she is stubborn enough to do it. I have never been separated from my twin for very long, and I'm not planning on starting now, but I also can't think of leaving here yet. I know what Caelius said, and I have confidence that he believes in what he said, but I still can't be certain that I'm the one.

What he told me about the other women and the men's gifts has me curious. I have never met anyone who could do anything similar to what Sara and I can do. That there are others like us and all living here happily cohabiting with each other using their gifts every day and being accepted fully has me thinking that maybe there is a life where we won't have to hide, where we won't have to be ashamed of people finding out that we are different.

"You aren't even listening to me." Sara's muttering finally penetrates my musings just as there is a knock on the door. "Who's that?" she asks with a raised brow as she looks at me.

I shake my head and make my way towards the door. Opening it a crack, I see two women standing there. One is holding a little boy's hand and the other is behind a pram with twins babbling away. "Hi. We came to introduce ourselves and welcome you to the compound." I open the door wider and see them looking at the two of us when Sara comes to stand next to me.

"Two?" the other one says. "Can they have two?" The women look at each other.

"I don't think so, but they are twins."

"What are the two of you talking about?" Sara suddenly asks with an impatient lift of her shoulder.

"Oh, sorry . . . it's just that we were expecting one of you," the one with the twins says just as we hear voices and three more women come strolling towards us. It looks like we are about to meet the women at the compound.

"Yay, we haven't missed anything," one of the new women says with a clap.

"There are two of them," the one with the boy reveals, and I see the others stop and look into the room.

"Wow, you go, Caelius," one with an impish look quips, and pumps her fist in the air.

"Nova!" one gasps, but then starts to laugh.

"Just ignore them," the one with the boy says with a big smile. "They're incorrigible."

"Hey . . . you're part of the gang too," Nova says cheekily as she leans forward and takes the boy in her arms. "Hello, my angel, have you missed me?" The boy nods with a toothless smile as he looks up at her happily.

"Anyway, I'm Jasmine, and that is my son, Orion."

"I'm Brielle, and I'm with Bion. If you aren't feeling well, he's the one to go see," she says with a happy smile.

"What she meant to say is if you're not feeling well, you can see either of them, because madam over here is just as good as her man. I'm Nova, by the way."

"I'm Gabriela, and this here is Talia. There are more of us. The others should be along any minute now. Can we come in?" I know I'm standing here with a bemused look on my face, but I don't know what to make of these women.

"Sure," I murmur, and step back, stepping on Sara's foot in the process.

"Ow!" she cries out as she jumps back. "Watch where you're going." I glare at her over my shoulder and then look forward again to see the women walking into the room.

"So what can we call you?" Talia asks with a raised brow as she takes a seat on the bed. Only now realizing that I haven't introduced us yet, I step forward.

"I'm Alaia, and this is my sister, Sara."

"What did we miss?" I snap around as I gasp at the voice of another woman behind me and see another three women standing there. All these women I have met today are beautiful. I feel drab standing here in my jeans, hoodie, and no shoes.

"One is Alaia, and the other one is Sara," Brielle says as she leans back against the headboard. "That there is Saskia, Aria, and Scarlett."

"Nice to meet all of you," I say with a smile, surprised at how friendly all of them are. I see Sara smile and nod in greeting, and then she moves towards the bed and sits cross-legged on the floor before them.

"So what kind of gift do you two have?"

At Brielle's question, Sara tenses and then jumps up and snaps around to look at me. I'm already holding my hands up in a motion of calmness.

"They're all the same as us, Sara. They all have gifts." At my answer, her eyes widen, and then she turns her head to the others and then back to me.

"Are you sure?" she whispers.

"Yes, I'm sure." That isn't really true, as I've only got Caelius's word on it, but deep down, I know he wouldn't lie to me. I look at the other women who are looking at the two of us questioningly. "I have a connection to nature. I can make things grow, even animals when their young are weak. I can help them." At my explanation, they look at each other.

"She will work well with you, Brielle. Both of you heal and nurture," Jasmine says excitedly. "I've been thinking we have pairs who have similar types of gifts even though they differ slightly."

"What do you mean?" Scarlett asks with a frown.

"Well, think about it. My gift and Gabriela's are different, but we both see things in the future. Aria and you, Scarlett, have similar gifts. What I'm trying to say is that I'm starting to see a pattern." At Jasmine's explanation, I see the nods and surprised looks on the women's faces.

"What about you, Sara? What gift have you got?"

At Talia's question, Sara looks at me again and then shrugs. "I can see people who are close to me, wherever they are, whatever they are doing at any time. I can see them," Sara explains.

"What I would like them to explain to me is how Caelius can have two. Maybe it's because they're twins," Nova says with a frown. I know what she's talking about, but I can see that Sara is completely confused with her statement.

"I'm the one with Caelius, not Sara," I reveal, which has the women nodding.

"Can you get trees and animals to do what you want?" Nova asks as she sits forward on the bed and places Orion on the floor so he can walk around.

"To a certain extent, yes," I reveal, which has Sara huffing.

"She's being modest. If you want something to grow overnight, just ask Alaia. If you want an animal, that no one else can tame, to behave, she's your girl. If you want weeds to come out of the ground and hold someone down, well, then, she's a pro with that one. I can profess to that." The women laugh at Sara's grumble, which has me smiling. When we were kids, it was my way of slowing her down when we were playing.

Suddenly, Nova claps her hands in excitement and looks around. "Do you know what this means?"

"Here comes trouble," Talia quips with a giggle, the others agreeing.

"Nothing too hectic, but what if Alaia has one of the guys tied down, or all of them?" she says happily. I know I'm smiling, and I shouldn't, as the men might be upset with the joke, but at the excitement on the women's faces, my imagination starts to create all different scenarios.

"Maybe we can do it at dinner tonight?" Gabriela says with a laugh. "What if we take her to the kitchen before the guys go in for dinner and she holds their chairs down?" At Gabriela's suggestion, I start to envision how to go about it.

"I don't know if that will work. You know how strong they are. They will tear those chairs apart," Brielle says with a frown.

"But the look on their faces will be priceless," Scarlett says. "I can't wait to see Cassius."

"I'm suddenly looking forward to dinner," Aria says with a laugh. "Shall we go start so that it's ready by the time they come in?" And with that comment, all the women prepare to leave, inviting us to accompany them. I have only met them a few minutes ago, but already I feel as if I know them; it has been Sara and I for the longest time. We have friends but always kept a barrier between us, feeling a separation between us because of our differences. With these women, I feel like we understand each other, like we have something in common.

"Do you think we can trust them?" Sara whispers as she walks next to me.

"They each have a gift of their own; I don't think there is any reason they would want to hurt us in any way." I go on to tell Sara about the gifts Caelius told me the women possessed and see her impressed look as she looks at the women who are now entering the kitchen. I see a huge wooden table near the entrance; I instantly look down at the chairs and smile when I see that the floor is a type of tile rock. I can bring the runners up from low in the ground and wrap them around the chairs' legs.

"What do you think? Can you do it?" Scarlett asks as she stands behind a chair. I look up at her and smile.

"Yes, I just need to know which chairs I need to tie down," I say as I look at the women's smiles. "Maybe we shouldn't do all of them today and do something else with the other men at some other time."

"I think that's a good idea, because once they suspect something is up, they won't be caught," Jasmine says.

"Well, let's only try three chairs, then," Talia says. "I think we should have Ceric, Bjarni, and Cassius." At the other women's confirmation, I'm shown which chairs to tie. An hour later, some are setting the table, others putting the final touches to dinner, when the men walk in. At the sound of male voices, I turn to find the men walking into the kitchen. If I weren't so infatuated with Caelius, I would be floored with these men. It is hard to choose which one is the best looking; these men are what women dream about when they talk about handsome.

"Pinch me," Sara says from next to me, which has me smiling like a loon until Caelius walks in and our eyes connect. I feel the colour rise in my cheeks, especially when Caelius's eyes travel over my body.

CAELIUS 6

When my eyes connect with hers, I can feel my muscles relaxing. The anger that was running through my body is now diminishing, and that feeling of belonging is surrounding me with its gentle hands. I know I owe this calmness to my woman. I see her face brighten with colour when she sees me looking at her. Her energy calls to me. I make my way towards her but stop when I see Ceric leaning down to kiss Nova on the forehead before he grabs his chair to pull it out.

Then Cassius also pulls at his chair, and it doesn't budge. He frowns. "What the fuck?" He pulls harder, and the wood cracks. Scarlett throws back her head and laughs in merriment when Cassius leans down to see what is holding the chair. I notice that Ceric has his hands low on his waist and is glaring at Nova suspiciously as she looks at him innocently.

"Nova?" Ceric grunts.

"What the hell?" Bjarni mutters as he pulls harder and trips back as the back of the chair breaks loose. All the women are now roaring with laughter, which has the men looking at them suspiciously, and then I see Alaia squatting and placing her hands on the ground. She closes her eyes for a few seconds and then stands. So, my woman likes to play pranks, does she?

"What the hell, Bjarni? You need to curb that strength of yours. Why did you break the chair?" Draco asks as he walks into the kitchen.

Bjarni looks at him with an exasperated look on his face. "It wasn't moving," he grunts.

Draco places his hand on the back of the chair that is still intact and slides it back effortlessly. He looks back at Bjarni and raises his eyebrow in question, which has Bjarni looking around at everyone suspiciously. Wulf, Burkhart, and Brandr are already sitting; therefore, they didn't play a prank on everyone, only on some. I glance at Nova and see her wink at Alaia, and I shake my head in amusement.

"Sit down or we will never eat," Nova says playfully to Ceric, who is still looking at the chair and then at Nova suspiciously. He takes hold of the chair again and effortlessly slides it out, which has him scowling, and then he goes down on his haunches to look under the table. "Would you like me to join you down there?" Nova leans over Ceric's chair and blows him a kiss.

"You're up to something, hellcat," Ceric says as he finally takes his chair, leans towards Nova, and takes her lips in a punishing kiss. "Behave."

I take the couple of steps left to reach Alaia and place my arm around her waist. The colour in her cheeks darken. Leaning down against her ear, I murmur, "I know it was you." When I stand back up, a cheeky smile is on her face. Before she can say anything, I kiss her moist lips. Her taste has images of our brief time together exploding in my mind. My cock hardens with anticipation as I feel her softness against me.

"Should we all leave?" Burkhart quips from where he's sitting with his arm around the back of Saskia's chair. Lifting my head, I just have time to see Saskia slapping his arm playfully, which has him grinning at her boyishly.

"Caelius, I don't want to rush you, but maybe when you come up for a breather, you would like to introduce everyone," Draco quips from the head of the table. Before leaving the meeting, Draco had congratulated me on finding my mate. I know all my brothers are happy for me. We all have each other's back; therefore, when there is something we don't have any control over, it becomes frustrating, such as not being able to find a brother's mate when we know he is struggling without her.

When Burkhart was looking for Saskia, we all went out of our way to try to find her because we knew she was close and didn't want to lose the opportunity of seeing Burkhart at peace and out of danger of turning into a Keres. When I saw Alaia's photo in a warehouse we raided a few months back and recognized her as my mate, my brothers tried to help me in every way to find her, and then when she was standing before me I hadn't even realized who she was, because I wasn't looking at her until I heard her voice.

Everything in me stilled, and then it all came rushing back. My senses were sharper. It felt like I could hear clearer, my sense of smell was purer, and my vision was more focused. I know that when an Elemental finds his mate, he becomes stronger mentally and physically, and the rage that eats at us as time goes past vanishes, but I never thought I would feel so invincible.

I look down at Alaia and incline my head towards Draco. "That there is Draco. He's the Elemental MC president," I introduce, and then to Draco and everyone around, I say, "This is Alaia, my mate, and this here is Sara, her sister."

"You're going to get them confused. If it weren't for their different clothes today, we would never have known who is who," Talia says as she serves a big helping of mash onto Celmund's plate.

"It is impossible for me to get her confused," I reply as I pull out Alaia's chair. I hear Sara's grunt of amusement.

"If we want to trick you, we will. Even our parents didn't recognize us when we wanted them not to." I don't tell her that it is physically impossible for me to get Alaia confused with her because I am repelled by any other female, even her twin sister, so I simply nod and stretch out my hand for the rolls, but I'm interrupted as one of our new prospects runs in.

"We have trouble," he states as he looks at Draco, and then we hear the beep of the alarm that Celmund has installed when there is a breach in the compound. Instantly, we are all on our feet, food forgotten, our only thought on protecting the women and children and destroying whoever thought they could enter without being invited. I feel Alaia's hand on mine before I can move away. Looking down, I see a concerned look on her face.

"Don't worry, you will be safe here," I state, trying to appease her. Leaning down, I kiss her forehead, and then follow the others out of the kitchen and towards whoever thought they could attack us. As we hurry into the garage, I hear the shutters descending. The women and children will be protected, and now it's time to fight.

"What's going on?" Draco asks of the new prospect as we start making our way outside.

"There were five men outside. They wanted to come in. When we denied them entrance, they created a scene insisting on entrance," he explains.

"Were there only five, and were they human?" Wulf asks as he looks around. After what happened with Sven and Gunner, we decided that all our prospects would be Elementals, except for the ones we already have, like Kade, who is Scarlett's brother, and Talia's brother, Jason.

"Yes, they were human, and there were only five of them wanting entrance."

Bjarni has squatted and has his hands on the ground, feeling for any vibration in the earth that might mean disturbance of the normal forest floor. "From the south," he grunts as he starts to make his way towards where he felt the vibrations.

"You, go back to your post," Draco orders of the prospect. "Burkhart, Caelius, Ceric, Bion, and I will follow Bjarni. The rest of you patrol around the compound." As soon as the words are out of Draco's mouth, we are off following after Bjarni. In no time, we are upon the five intruders. We have them surrounded and at gunpoint before they even know what is happening.

"Why are you on our land?" Draco asks calmly.

"They wouldn't let us in," one of them argues.

"Well, that should have told you that we don't want strangers on our land," Draco says as he approaches the men.

"We don't want any trouble. We just want the women back." At his words, I frown. Which women is he looking for? Saskia's friends are no longer with us, so it can't be them. Are they looking for Alaia and Sara?

"And what women might you be referring to?" Draco asks with a bored expression on his face.

"I know they're here. Sara had a tracker that I planted on her hoodie." At his words, I tense. If these fuckers think they are going to take my woman anywhere, they have another thing coming.

"They are now under our protection," Draco says with a raised brow. "Therefore, you will be escorted to the gate, and you can leave. Don't ever come back without an invitation." He starts to turn, when one of them jumps at him. Bad idea. Draco has him face down on the ground with his boot pressing behind his neck before any of them can even blink. "Anyone else want to try that?"

"They are my sisters; I just want to make sure they are fine. I know you're not the ones who were after them initially, so I suspect you are helping them. Please," one of the guys to my right says. I look at him closely and realize that he does have a slight resemblance to the twins.

"Caelius?" At Draco's unasked question, I nod. He wants confirmation that this guy in fact is the twins' brother. "Fine, you can talk to them, but once you see that they are safe, you can leave. Trust me when I say that this is the safest place for them at the moment." He lifts his foot and starts to stride away.

"We are just as able to keep them safe," the guy Draco subdued snaps. Draco ignores him and continues walking. "Pompous asshole." Suddenly, he's on his back again, but this time, Burkhart is above him.

"You can't even protect yourself, fucker. How do you expect to protect a woman?" Burkhart grunts as he leans down and pulls the guy's head back by his hair. "You're lucky you're still breathing. I hear another sound coming out of you, and you won't be breathing any longer." With that warning, he steps away from him and shakes his head in disgust. "Now let's get moving or your opportunity to see the women will be gone."

The others start to make their way towards the compound. I step next to Alaia's brother and incline my head so that he will start walking. "Are they okay?" he asks, and I can hear the concern in his voice.

"Yes, they are fine, and I know they will be pleased to see you." We don't talk the rest of the way, but I can tell that what I said to him has appeased his concern. When we reach the outside of the compound, we find Draco and Wulf standing by the door to the bar area. My eyes connect with Draco's, and I know the women have been advised to join us. I know Alaia is now mine, but I haven't been with her long enough for her to realize that she will be happy here.

If they want to leave, will I be able to let her go? Instantly, my anger rises with such force that I know that I won't. I can't have her in danger, but I also can't have her where I can't see her. Our bond will prevent us from being far from each other for too long. We enter the bar area, and Ceric points to the tables on the far side. The men suspiciously make their way there.

I sense Alaia before I see her. The minute she walks through the door with Sara, I can see the concern on her face. Her eyes clash with mine as she walks in, a frown marring her forehead. I want to go to her and appease her concern, but I hold back, as I don't want her brother to feel the need to take her away. I incline my head to my left so that she can see why she's been called. Her eyes widen when she sees her brother, and then she rushes towards him. My first instinct is to hold her back, keep her safe, but I don't move.

My hands are fisted so tightly that I'm sure a bone will snap soon if I don't relax. I feel a hand on my shoulder, and I look to my right to see Wulf standing there nonchalantly. I know he's silently letting me know that he understands my predicament.

"Joshua," Sara says excitedly as she hugs her brother. Alaia stands behind her with a smile on her face. When Sara finally moves away, Joshua pulls Alaia into his arms in a hug, but that's when I lose my self-control. I take a step towards them, but the hand that Wulf had on my shoulder is now around my upper arms, and Bjarni is standing before me.

"Don't do it, Brother," Bjarni says quietly, way too low for anyone to be able to hear. I know he means well, but all I can see is Alaia in another man's arms. "He's her brother and will soon leave. If you make a scene, she might want to leave with him." My heart is beating erratically, my vision tunnelling.

"How about you all sit down and talk? Once you're happy that they are fine, you can leave," Bion says to Joshua, who steps back and once again takes his seat, which has my muscles relaxing slightly. I see Bion guiding Alaia and Sara to chairs, but then Alaia stops suddenly and looks back over her shoulder at me, a frown again on her face. She turns and heads towards me, a soft look on her face.

"Excuse me," she murmurs to Bjarni, who looks over his shoulder. After a few seconds, he steps away, and Alaia approaches me. Her hand lifts, and she places it on my chest, her eyes soft as she looks up at me. "What's wrong?" she asks quietly, a worried look on her face. I know she can feel animals and the vegetation around her, but how can she feel my agitation? It's still too soon for her to be able to sense my feelings.

"What do you mean, kitten?" I can feel the warmth of her hand through my T-shirt and the feeling of calm that is spreading through my body.

"Why are you so angry?" she murmurs softly, her hand now gently stroking my chest.

"I know he's your brother, but I don't like seeing other men touching you." I will never lie to her, and even though she might be upset with the reason for my anger, I need her to know the reason for it.

ALAIA 7

His revelation for the reason of his anger surprises me. When I started to feel the agitation and anger coming from somewhere, I knew it was from Caelius, because I've realized that there is an internal nurturing feeling that I have towards him that I have never had with anyone or anything else. That he was so angry because of jealousy has me flabbergasted, but then I remember the episode when we were sitting in the kitchen and how blinded with jealousy I was when Sara bragged about being able to trick Caelius to think she was me. The thought of Caelius touching Sara in any way thinking that it could be me blinds me with anger.

"It's okay, I understand." At my words, I see his eyes widen in surprise, and then his hand comes up and covers mine as I stroke his chest soothingly.

"You calm me," he whispers before he lowers his head and kisses me gently on the lips, but suddenly, his lips are gone and so is he. My head snaps around when I feel my back to someone and realize that Caelius has me behind his back. How did he move so quickly? I turn and understand when I see Joshua standing before him with a furious look on his face. I feel a knot in my stomach at the anger radiating from both men.

"My sister isn't one of your playthings," Joshua says angrily as he comes to stand before Caelius. "I'm taking them with me." I can see Caelius's muscles tense in anger at Joshua's statement. I try to step around Caelius, and instantly, his arm moves behind him and he holds me around my waist against his back.

I place my hands flat on his back to try to calm him, but I can feel the anger flowing through his tense muscles. "Alaia is not going anywhere," Caelius grunts, which has Joshua taking in a deep breath.

"Stop it," I say angrily as I look around Caelius's back. "Joshua, stop it. I know you're trying to protect me, but I want to be here." At my statement, I see Joshua shake his head in anger, his hands fisted at his sides.

"How can you want to be here if you only met this son of a bitch today? Is he threatening you in any way?" At Joshua's question, I feel Caelius's body vibrate with anger. I place my arms around his arms, knowing that he is ready to explode into violence.

"I would never threaten Alaia. I will protect her with my life," Caelius states in a threatening voice that has me worrying about a fight breaking out because of me.

"Is it so difficult to believe that I want to be with him? That he's the one I want?"

"You don't know what you want. You've only met him," Joshua argues as he lifts his hand in agitation.

"I do know. Trust me when I say I know."

"You're coming with me. You don't know them from anywhere. They could be in cahoots with the others," Joshua says angrily.

"Don't compare us to the Keres," Caelius growls in anger.

"Caelius," I call softly, and he looks over his shoulder at me. "Let me talk to him by myself. It will be okay." I see the anger in his beautiful eyes, and he shakes his head at my request. "Please, you said I could talk to him." He squeezes his eyes for a few seconds, but then he finally opens them and nods. I lift up on my toes and kiss him gently on the lips. "Thank you." And then I step away from him and before Joshua. "Let's go sit down and talk about this," I say. Not waiting for his reply, I make my way towards the chair I was going to sit on previously, Sara following us.

I know Caelius is still where I left him and that he is going to stay there until I'm done. I believe that no matter what, he will keep to his word. I don't know about Joshua, though, as he has a hot temper and is stubborn. When he thinks of something, it is difficult to change his mind.

"What do you think you're doing?" Joshua growls as he sits before me. "The day you get here, you sleep with one of them. They're fucking bikers, Alaia."

I can feel the anger radiating up my legs from the ground. I know it's coming mostly from Caelius. "These bikers helped us and got us away from the Keres," I argue, trying to keep my voice down so our conversation can't be heard by the others.

"That doesn't mean you have to sleep with them," he growls angrily.

"You make it sound as if she's sleeping around," Sara mutters angrily as she looks around warily. That's one thing about Sara and I—we might not agree about certain things, but when it comes down to it, we have each other's back.

"Isn't she? She's been here one day and already she's slept with that one. Who's going to be next?" I gasp in surprise at Joshua's cruel words. I know he's saying that because he's worried about me, but he has never been so cruel. I hear a commotion to my right and look over to see Bjarni and Wulf holding Caelius back.

"It's time you left," Ceric says as he comes to stand before Joshua, a frown on his face.

"I'm not done," Joshua answers angrily.

"That's too bad. You either leave now or you don't leave at all. We won't be able to hold him back for long." At Ceric's words, I look over at Caelius again and notice that Bion is also before him now.

"Who, him?" Joshua asks as he points at Caelius. "Let him come. I'm not scared of him." He shrugs.

I stand and pick up my hands in supplication as I face Joshua again. "Joshua, I know you're worried about us, but you can see that we are safe here. Please, once we are safe, we will contact you and come home," I plead anxiously, trying to get them to leave, as I can feel the fury radiating from him.

"I'm not leaving without the two of you. After what I saw, I think it's time that we get you another place to hide," he grunts angrily.

"Don't be stubborn; you know this is the best place for us, Josh. We're not going anywhere until we know we're safe, and as you can see, we are completely safe, and in case you haven't noticed, we're both twenty-four-year-olds who can decide for ourselves who we sleep with," Sara says as she stands. I know Joshua won't back down, so I shrug and start to walk away.

"Where are you going, Alaia?" Joshua asks angrily, but I ignore him and continue making my way towards Caelius. I hear a noise behind me, but I don't look around as I approach Caelius, Bion, and Bjarni.

"I'm going inside now. Do you want to come with me?" I see that Caelius's concentration is behind me, and I know it's on my brother. "Caelius!" I call, but he doesn't look at me. I slide around Bion and place my hand on his arm. "Caelius, look at me." His eyes snap to mine, and I see the fury in them.

"Come with me," I whisper.

"He can't talk to you like that." His voice is a deep growl.

"Come with me. It's over. He's just worried and doesn't know how to deal with it not being him protecting us." I see the fight he's going through. "Please." At my plea, I know he won't deny me.

"Go with your woman, Brother. We will see them out," Wulf says from behind Caelius. I incline my head towards the back door and see him nod slightly. Bjarni doesn't let go of Caelius but loosens his grip as we move towards the back door. Once we're through the door, Bjarni lets go and stands with his arms crossed in the doorway. Him and Caelius look at each other for a few minutes, and then Bjarni inclines his head in a slight nod as if a silent message was passed between the two of them.

I place my hand in Caelius's and feel his fingers close over my hand. I start to walk into the compound and towards the courtyard. Suddenly, I'm against the wall and Caelius is over me. "I know he's your brother, but I can't let anyone speak to you like that." I can hear the anger in his voice as he lowers his head and then takes my lips in a blistering kiss.

We are still kissing a few minutes later, when someone clears their throat. "I hate to interrupt, but can we speak?" When I hear Sara, I tense. I know she doesn't agree with Caelius and me either, but I also know she won't talk about Joshua in front of anyone, as Josh is family. Caelius looks over his shoulder at her and then back at me. The last thing I want at the moment is to talk to Sara, but I know I need to tell her something.

I place my hand on his chest. "Will you give us a second?" He looks deep into my eyes for a couple seconds and then nods and turns. I look at him walking into the courtyard and then stopping to talk to Aria and Saskia.

"You know that Joshua was right, don't you?" Sara says from next to me, which has me turning my head and concentrating on her.

"Sara, he is meant for me." At her rolling of the eyes, I continue. "You know how my gift works, with me feeling the rightness of the earth, the vibrations around me?" She nods at my question, a frown on her face.

"Well, this is the same; I can feel the rightness, Sara. I know without any doubt that he is the one for me." At my explanation, I see her struggle to understand and believe, but after a minute, she nods hesitantly.

"You know I will always have your back, and above everyone else, I trust your instinct. Therefore, if you say you believe he is the one for you, then I believe you." I pull her towards me and hug her close.

"Thank you, sis," I murmur.

"Well, you better go. With a man like that at your disposal, I wouldn't be hanging around hugging my sister," she jokes as she takes a step back and inclines her head in Caelius's direction, which has me smiling cheekily before I make my way towards this man whom until a day ago, I didn't know. What I said to Sara is the truth; not only was I convinced with a tattoo that appeared from nowhere, but I feel an overwhelming nurturing feeling that is stronger than anything I have ever felt with the earth.

Caelius turns towards me as I approach, his eyes traveling the length of my body, making my cheeks heat with passion. His body is a work of art that has my hands itching to stroke over his chest. He lifts his hand, placing it behind my neck as he pulls me towards him, his lips descending to cover mine in a blistering kiss that has both of us forgetting everyone and everything around us.

The heat pools between my legs in anticipation of his touch. His fingers entwine in my hair as he holds my head still as his tongue plays with mine. I can feel his hardness against me, professing to his passion, his maleness overwhelming my senses. I want to slide my hands down over his stomach to his jeans and stroke over the bulge that drove all thoughts out of my mind. Taste the wetness that dribbles down his length.

"Woah, get a fire extinguisher," Saskia teases as Caelius lifts his head, my cheeks heating in embarrassment. I hear footsteps behind me and look over my shoulder to see Burkhart and Brandr approaching.

"It's time," Brandr says when he stops across from me and pulls Aria into his arms.

"Time for what?" Saskia asks as Burkhart kisses her forehead.

"We know where Vercin is, and we're going to attack tonight. Draco has updated Jasmine so that you ladies can help us." At Cassius's comment, I look up in surprise to Caelius. What are the women going to help with and what does he mean with attack?

"Are you ready?" Draco calls from the entrance to the courtyard, his hands low on his waist, a frown on his face. Draco has a look about him that has all the women sighing after him, but there is an aura of danger surrounding him that clearly states he is alpha. Caelius bends his head again and kisses me lightly on the lips.

"The other women will let you know what's happening. I will see you later." And with those words, he steps away and leaves. I look at the other women and see their concerned looks. The word attack has me concerned.

"What is going on?" I ask.

"Vercin is the Keres president, and our men have been trying to catch him for centuries," Aria says, which has me frowning.

"What do you mean for centuries?" At my question, I see both women look at each other and then back at me.

"Did Caelius tell you he's different?" Saskia asks as she rubs a finger over her bottom lip.

"Yes."

"The thing about being an Elemental is that they have long lives," Aria says as she takes my hand and starts to pull me behind her, Saskia walking next to us.

"How long are we talking about?" I can already feel a knot growing in my stomach. What will happen when I start to get old and Caelius is still looking as fit as ever?

"Let's say they're centuries old," Saskia reveals, which has me catching my breath.

"Breathe," Aria says with a laugh.

"He said they only have one mate in their lives, but how is that possible if we die?" We walk into an area that looks like it could be an entertainment room.

"He didn't tell you? How could he not have told you the best perk of all?" Nova says suddenly from inside. I notice all the women are already here and have started talking at Nova's statement.

"What do you mean?"

"Well, sweetie, you now live as long as your man does too," Gabriela says happily.

They must be joking. "Are you saying I'm going to live forever?"

"Well, you're going to live as long as your man does," Talia says as she comes to stand before me with a smile. "He's been living for centuries, so it's prudent to think he knows how to take care of himself."

"I'm surprised Burkhart is still alive," Saskia grumbles. "That man doesn't know the concept of being careful," I see Brielle pat her arm playfully.

"Don't despair; I think Ceric was more in danger of losing his life when Nova saw his room for the first time than Burkhart has ever been." The women all laugh at Brielle's quip, which leaves me confused, but Talia quickly explains to me that Ceric had a collection of sex toys in his room that rivalled any sex shop when Nova came here.

"Shall we start? I would like to make sure that everything is safe before the men get there," Jasmine interrupts, which has everyone quickly agreeing and moving towards her. I look around confused, when Talia takes my hand.

"Come on, the first time is a bit scary, but then it gets better." At her words, I frown. What is she talking about?

"What are we doing?" I ask, and Brielle and Scarlett frown before they shrug.

"Jasmine guides us in finding Vercin. After that, we use our gifts to stop them or slow them down any way we can," Gabriela says. "All you need to do is place your hand on Jasmine and don't let go until we're all done."

This is definitely something I wasn't expecting. Is this like an ouija board but with a person? "How do I know when she finds Vercin?"

"Don't worry, just close your eyes and let yourself go," Saskia guides, which has me reluctantly stretching out my hand and touching Jasmine lightly on her neck. I see the other women close their eyes. I'm reluctant to try this, as I don't know what exactly is going to happen, but I close my eyes and wait. I have my eyes closed for a few minutes and am about to open them, sure that when I do, the women will all start laughing at my gullibility, when an image explodes in my mind.

It's so clear that I'm sure I gasp in surprise; it's as if I'm in the same room as them. I actually feel the need to run and hide, but then I feel the evilness shooting up my legs, and I know that these are the men who were after me. My curiosity has the better of me, and I step closer, sure that they can't see me, because by now, they would have seen me already, but just in case, I lean down and touch my hands to the ground, asking for the earth's help in holding these men down if I need it.

Once I get a feeling of warmth flowing through my hands, I know that my wish has been granted. Stepping closer, I see the men looking at a drawing on the table. Just then, a woman walks into the room, her long red hair tied back in a ponytail. "They are on their way," she says as she approaches the table. "Are you ready to leave? The place in Stellenbosch has been prepared?"

They are leaving? We need to warn the guys, but before I can open my eyes, their next words stop me.

"Is everything in place? We need to get as many of them as possible, and then we can get the women," one man asks the woman.

"The sensors are in place. Whoever comes into the house will be blown away," the woman states as she moves towards the drawing and points. "One bomb is here. The other one has been placed under the floorboards over there." The man stands and nods, and then he steps around the woman and walks towards the door.

"Make sure those fucking Elementals die. I'm tired of this cat-and-mouse game. I will not be pleased if you miss," he rasps before he leaves.

My heart is racing. What if we don't warn them in time? I struggle to open my eyes, but when I do, I see that most of the women's eyes are already open and they all have a worried look on their faces.

"We . . ." I start to talk, but Scarlett elbows me gently and shakes her head. I see that everyone is still touching Jasmine; therefore, I keep my position and mouth to Scarlett that we need to warn the men. She nods and then looks around to find Nova. She inclines her head in her direction, and I see that Nova has her phone out and is texting with her free hand.

I hope the men get the message and stop in time. I don't know what I just saw or how I saw it, but I know that if I can stop these men from getting hurt, then I will do anything in my power to help.

CAELIUS 8

We are nearly at our destination when Celmund tells us to turn back. We have our coms in; therefore, we hear the conversation between Draco and Celmund. Apparently the women found that this was a setup. Celmund still didn't know all the details but was asked to tell us not to go. We have all turned our bikes and are on our way back to the compound.

We are all ready for a fight, so to have to turn around when we're on our way to kill that son of a bitch has all our tempers up. We all trust the women. Every single piece of advice they have given us has been correct. They have saved our lives a few times, and to be honest, we are all very lucky to have such courageous women amongst us.

I believe Alaia will fit in perfectly. I know we haven't spoken about the future or what life is like living among us at the compound, but I have seen a streak of courage from Alaia that gives me hope that she will withstand any storm that might rise and that she will stand next to me as my woman, my lover, my confident, my best friend.

"I want everyone in the computer room," Draco says as we park our bikes. I can feel the anger that everyone is holding at bay. Every time we go out to stop the Keres, we get worked up, sure that we will make a difference and make it better for the other Elementals. When we started to realize what our women could do, hope was born that maybe they would be able to help the Elementals who were near changing.

Till now, they have been helping us find the Keres on some of our missions, but Celmund has been tasked with informing everyone if there is an Elemental nearing his change. We have been warned of two brothers who are showing signs of changing; we have organized to have them come here so that Brielle and the other women can try helping them.

"Are the women in the computer room?" I hear Wulf asking, and get Celmund's affirmative answer. I make my way towards the room, wanting to know how Alaia did with her first time with the women. I'm also feeling the need to touch my woman. I think because we haven't been bonded for long, the need to be close to her, to protect her, is uppermost on my mind. I have a need for her that I have never felt before in my life. When we are together, the feelings that surround me calm my mind, a mind that has been in turmoil since I was caught.

I enter the computer room and find Alaia standing next to Nova and Ceric. I walk towards them and place my arms around my kitten's midriff, pulling her against me. Instantly, the feeling of peace surrounds me. Alaia looks up at me, her face darkening with a blush as she smiles. "I'm so glad you guys were warned in time," she murmurs.

"Let's all take our places so that we can get to the bottom of this and make a plan," Draco states as he leans back in his chair. Bjarni and Gabriela are the last to take their seats after settling the twins in their prams. Everyone quietens, waiting for Draco to start.

"What happened?" he asks without wasting any time. Draco is the only one who knows Vercin personally. Before becoming a Keres, Vercin was Draco's rival, and after that, when he became a Keres, they continued as rivals, but Vercin made it a personal vendetta to create a team that would be better than the Elementals MC, and that's why he started the Keres MC. Centuries ago, the Keres were easier to control, but since Vercin, they have become a killing machine that we have to fight constantly.

Vercin has made it a war between us. Before, we knew that if we turned Keres, it was surely death. But since Vercin gave the Keres the opportunity to do his evil deeds, we have had a constant war on our hands.

"Vercin was leaving," Scarlett reveals. "They were preparing his chopper."

"They had sensors and bombs," Nova says as she leans back against Ceric. He places his hand over her baby bump and strokes as he lowers his head and kisses her neck in comfort.

"They knew you were coming," Aria says as she shrugs. I see Draco look over at Celmund and raise an eyebrow.

"The intel we got was from their communication, which means they know we are listening in on them," Celmund says with a frown.

"Once again we lose him," Wulf grunts as he strokes Jasmine's hand.

"Well," Alaia says as she looks around. I can feel her tense body beneath my hand. I squeeze her shoulder gently to give her the support she seems to need. "I heard the woman say that the place in Stellenbosch was ready for the man to go to."

I sit forward and look over at Celmund as he starts to type away. Draco also sits forward as he nods and looks around. "Is there anything else that can point to where we can find him?"

"I kept seeing an image of a shopping centre when I touched one of them. It didn't make sense at the time, but now it does," Gabriela says, which has Bjarni growling in anger.

"Why are you touching them?" I see his arms bulging as he glares at his woman.

"It's not as if he can feel me touching him, baby. He didn't even know I was there," Gabriela argues as she shrugs.

"You—"

"Enough. You can continue this discussion after we have the information we need," Draco grunts as he stands. "Gabriela, please continue." I now understand the other brothers' anger every time their women look or even touch some other man. The thought of Alaia looking at another man has my anger rising.

"Umm, sorry . . ." Gabriela mutters as she glares at Bjarni, who glares back at her. "I kept seeing a shopping centre and then a basement. I now think that might be where Vercin is going to be hiding next."

"Do you know the name of the shopping centre?" Celmund asks as he looks up from his laptop.

"I'm not sure. I think there was something that said square, but I didn't see the rest," Gabriela says as she shakes her head.

"Stellenbosch Square," Talia says suddenly. "I've been there a few times before." Celmund leans forward and kisses Talia hard on the lips before he sits back and winks at her before he starts to type on his laptop again. A moment later, he is turning the laptop around and presenting it to Gabriela.

"Look at those images and see if you recognize any of them."

Gabriela leans forward as she looks at the images, and then she points to one of them. "That one. I remember that," she says as she points towards an image of a parking lot with the shopping centre behind. Celmund nods and takes his laptop back as he continues to type away.

"Is there anything else?" Draco asks as he looks around.

"Yes," Jasmine says as she looks back at Wulf. "Katya was with them." At her words, he tenses. Jasmine looks forward at everyone and then at Draco. "Is she going to be a problem again?" Katya has always been a thorn in Wulf's side since he met Jasmine. For a long time now, we haven't heard anything from her, but it seems Jasmine still doesn't like the idea of her being anywhere near her man.

"No, sweetheart, she's not going to be a problem," Draco promises, which has Jasmine nodding. Wulf places his arm around her shoulders and pulls her close against his chest.

"There is Keres activity at the shopping centre. I think we should get eyes on there," Celmund says as he continues to look at his laptop. I'm sure he is looking at the cameras at the centre and is already seeing all the movement there.

"Can't they see that you are onto them again?" Talia asks as she looks at Celmund.

"Now that I know how they were duping us, I have covered my tracks, so no, they can't."

"Should we look into the shopping centre and try to see what is going on?" Brielle asks with a raised brow.

"Of course," Nova says before anyone else can confirm, which has most of the men shaking their heads in amusement.

"The one guy, who now I think is Vercin, when he spoke about the bomb going off and killing all the men, he mentioned that after all of you are dead, they can get the women," Alaia says, which has most of us swearing angrily. Those sons of bitches are still after our women. It will be a cold day in hell when they get their hands on any of us.

"That doesn't make sense, though," Aria says as she inclines her head. "If you guys die, then we won't survive for much longer, now will we?"

"There must be something he wants. There must be something you can maybe do that he knows about that we don't," Brandr says with a frown.

"We have thought about that, but what could it be?" Talia says as she looks at Celmund. "Jasmine did have a point that we have similar gifts within our group that enhance each other, but I don't see how that could do anything."

"In what way?" Burkhart asks as he strokes Saskia's hair, which has her closing her eyes.

"If you look at Brielle, she can heal and calm. Also, if you look at Alaia, she can nourish and grow. If you put them together, you have the perfect healing. Same goes for Aria, who can read thoughts, Nova, who can persuade, and Scarlett, who can tell the truth. Each of these gifts enhances the other."

I had never thought about it like this, but it makes sense. If each of them enhances the other's gift when they work together, then it means that they can acquire even more results then they were getting before. Then I tense when I think of an option. Is it possible?

"What if they can reverse the fury of the Keres now with Alaia, and Vercin knows somehow?" At my question, everyone looks at me, surprised, and then they all start talking at the same time.

"Enough," Draco mutters, but everyone quickly quietens as he stands. "Get me a Keres." He looks at Gunner. "And put him in the cell." If this is true, we can help all the Keres we capture except the ones who have had mates, because I doubt we can help those.

"If this works, how are we going to maintain them as Elementals?" Gabriela asks with a frown. "Because won't they just turn again if we don't know who their mates are?"

"Celmund and I can try the energy meter that we have been working on; we just need to figure out a way to send out the signal," Bion says as he looks over at Celmund, who nods.

"Ladies, I'm going to get a Keres here. Will you try to change him back?" Draco asks as he looks around the table. Alaia looks back at me with a question in her eyes, and I nod, which has her nodding and looking forward again.

"I'm able to revitalize animals and plant, but I've never tried with people," Alaia says, which has Draco looking at her and then at Brielle.

"Bion, Caelius, and Celmund, when we have the Keres, I want you to work with the women to see what they can do," Draco states. "The rest of us need to figure out what Vercin is up to. If he knows something, then I want to know what it is." It's the first time Draco has the women and men working together as a whole. He has asked the women for help before, but we haven't necessarily worked together.

"If the women start to explore what they can do in pairs and maybe bring it to the group as they usually do, I think there is much more they haven't even tapped into yet," Cassius comments as he looks at Scarlett.

"This is exciting," Nova comments with a grin, which has Ceric shaking his head in amusement.

"Let's get to it, then," Draco grunts as he walks out of the room. I look over at Wulf and see him frowning at Draco's departure. Draco is on edge, something that worries all of us.

"What's up?" Bjarni asks as he, too, looks at Wulf. Wulf looks around at everyone and shrugs, also standing. He pulls Jasmine up from her chair and guides her to where Orion is playing before kissing her on the lips lightly.

"I'll speak to him," he says before he also leaves the room. We have all found our mates except for Draco, and that worries us all, because he is the oldest of the Elementals, and there is no one stronger than him, but even with the strongest willpower, he has to fight his inner self constantly to not change.

"We need to find his mate," I mumble, but it's loud enough for all the other brothers to hear.

ALAIA 9

It has been two days since the meeting, and in those two days, we have all been looking at different ways of using our gifts. Even Sara has been helping; I've noticed some tension between her and Gunner and suspect that the two of them are attracted to each other but are fighting it for some reason. I've tried to ask her, but she says I'm imagining things, which clearly indicates to me that she's not willing to speak about it yet. I've also asked Sara to keep checking on Joshua just to make sure he is fine and doesn't try anything, like trying to take us out of here.

I know he doesn't understand this connection I have with Caelius, but maybe one day, when we're not still hiding from the Keres, I can explain the way I feel to him without telling him about what Caelius really is. The few days we have had together have been the most intense days I have ever had in my life; he is caring, understanding, and gentle. When he is close to me, I feel invincible.

"They have a Keres in the cell," Brielle says as she walks into the kitchen where I'm having breakfast with Scarlett and Talia. "Are you ready to try what we have been planning?" Brielle and I have sat together and discussed our gifts and what we know we can do and what we might be able to still do. We decided that when they captured a Keres, we would try to help them and see until what point we are able to reverse their anger.

"Sure, if we can do this, it will be great. We must just make sure that Nova and Aria are ready to listen to his thoughts and persuade him to be calm until hopefully the others can find his mate or a solution to keeping him calm." I never thought I would be doing something like this, much less working towards helping others. I stand and take my plate to the sink. Rinsing it out, I place it on the counter before I turn and make my way towards Brielle, who is talking to the other women. I wonder if we should call Caelius and Bion before we try to work with the Keres, but I'm sure there must be someone there by him.

"Shall we go?" I ask, which has all three women standing. I smile because I should have realized that they would want to be there to see what happens. We make our way to the cell area and find no one there except a man inside the cell. As soon as we enter, I can feel the evilness rising through the floor and up my legs. Nausea engulfs me with the hate this man carries within him. When he sees us, his face turns into a scowl and he growls like a captured animal.

"Hello," Brielle says, but we don't approach, as we know how unpredictable the Keres can be.

"I'm not a fucking monkey for you to come and appease your curiosity with," he roars in anger as he charges against the bars. We all jump back in fright at his angry outburst.

"We're not here to appease our curiosity. We want to help you," Talia says, which has the guy snorting angrily and hitting the wall with an open palm.

"Help?" he says sarcastically. "Okay, if you are here to help, then why don't you open this cell so I can get out and thank you personally."

"Lie. If we open the door, you will try to kill all of us," Scarlett says.

"Why did you become a Keres?" Talia asks with a raised brow.

"Why don't you mind your fucking business? I don't see how that has anything to do with you."

"True," Scarlett says, and looks at Talia with a shrug. It doesn't look like we are going to be able to help him if he doesn't calm. I squat down until I'm touching the ground and place my hands flat on the floor. I then close my eyes and ask the earth to surround him and calm him enough so that we can help him.

I then look up at Brielle. "Do you want to try to send some of your healing energy through my connection with the earth until he is calm enough for us to be able to touch?" At my question, Brielle leans forward and places her hands on my shoulders. I instantly feel her energy penetrating my being and filling me with warmth and calmness. A few seconds later, roots start spreading from the top of the cell, coming in through slight cracks in the rock. He still hasn't seen them as he stands against the bars, glaring at us suspiciously.

They move quickly down the walls until they're near enough to climb up his legs and hold him still. He starts to struggle and pulls a few loose, but they are moving too fast for him to be completely free, and soon, he is tied down and roaring in anger. He fights and screams, but to no use, as soon, he isn't able to move at all, and after a few minutes, his breathing also calms. I once again close my eyes and start seeing myself helping him calm, helping him find his path back to himself.

This is something I have done before but only with animals. I have never done this with a human being, but according to the others, my gift would have expanded in different aspects after bonding with Caelius, and the only way for me to find out how is to try it.

I see myself surrounded in a pink light, and then that light is flowing through my hands and towards the man in the cell. I imagine that light flowing up his legs until he is surrounded. I then feel my love surrounding him and comforting him. My eyes are looking at him, but I'm not seeing him. I am seeing the pink light comforting him, the light that will be filling his heart with love instead of hate, with hope instead of loss.

The hate and anger that he carries seeps deep into my bones. I feel the tears flowing down my cheeks at the despair I feel. "He's draining them. I'm going to help, maybe call the others," I hear Scarlett say as if from far away. I realize that this fury of his that we are trying to reverse into happiness is too deep. I can feel myself weakening and Brielle's energy stuttering as she also tries to keep on healing him. Then I feel Scarlett's hand touching me, a warmth enveloping me, and even though I don't feel stronger, at least I don't feel myself draining as quickly.

I don't know how long we are like that. I can feel that I'm about to pass out, when I hear a commotion, and then a blast of energy fills me. Before I can pass out, I send the flux of energy towards the man, and then darkness surrounds me.

"Fuck," I hear Cassius roar. "I'm going to kill that son of a bitch."

Why is he so upset?

"Alaia!" Is that Caelius? His voice sounds rough, as if he's having difficulty talking. And then I feel arms around me, and I know he has picked me up. Realization suddenly comes to me, and I struggle to open my eyes. When I do, I encounter Caelius's chest. Turning my head slightly, I notice that Cassius is sitting on the floor with Scarlett on his lap. Bion is walking out the door with Brielle. All I see is his tense muscles. My eyes flicker up, and I see the anger in Caelius's face.

Why are they all so angry?

"I need to persuade him before all of this was for nothing," I hear Nova say.

"I don't fucking like this, hellcat," Ceric says.

"That's too bad, as it has to be done," she mutters, and then I see her walking closer to the cell, Ceric right next to her.

"Kitten?" My eyes flicker up to Caelius's, and I see concern in them. "How are you feeling?" At his question, I realize how tired I'm feeling. My body and mind are completely exhausted. Usually I feel a little drained, but at the moment, I'm totally exhausted.

"Just tired, just need to rest," I murmur, already snuggling into his arms.

"Why didn't you call us?" he asks as he starts to make his way out of the cell area.

"Wait," I grumble, and feel Caelius tense as he stops, a frown on his face. "We can't leave. I might need to calm him." He is shaking his head before I even finish talking.

"You're not doing anything else or I'm going to kill him if you lose consciousness again," Caelius grunts angrily.

"We need to make sure that it works or not. Otherwise, we will have to do it all over again." I can feel how tense Caelius is and how his anger is vibrating through him. He turns and walks back into the cell area. I hear Nova talking to the Keres, and Aria is next to her. I know Nova is persuading the Keres to keep calm and Aria is listening to his thoughts to make sure that what we did is working.

"I don't want you to do that shit again," I hear Cassius arguing. "Keres are all lies. They will eat you alive if you let them."

"I had to do something; Brielle and Alaia were fading fast," Scarlett says as she leans against Cassius. I see the Keres shaking his head as he looks around. Nova has stopped talking, but Aria is still looking at him intently. I hope this has worked, because if it didn't, I don't know what else we can do.

Aria looks around until she finds me. "His thoughts aren't as angry, but I don't think he has changed yet." I feel a knot in my stomach at the disappointment of not changing him. "We will have to try again." At her words, the men all growl in anger just as Draco, Wulf, and Bjarni walk in.

"I'm taking it that the experiment didn't work," Draco says as he walks towards the cell.

"I didn't say that. It worked, but there is still some anger in him."

"Alaia, Brielle, and Scarlett were passed out," Cassius mutters. "They are going to have to find another way because it clearly effects them." Draco looks at Scarlett and then at me with a concerned look on his face.

"Are they okay?" he asks as he looks at Caelius, who nods, and then Cassius, who reluctantly nods too. "Is there another way?"

"I don't know," Aria says as she looks at Nova, and then her eyes snap to mine, as I'm sure she's reading my mind. "Maybe there is." She nods at me.

"I think that it didn't work fully because our energy wasn't combined. We were quickly drained, but when

Scarlett joined us, I felt the strength that came through," I murmur, my eyes fighting to close with my exhaustion.

"Do you want to try it again?" Draco asks me.

"Fuck, Draco," Caelius grunts angrily, but I place my hand on his cheek as I look up at him. His eyes snap down to mine, and we stand like that for a few seconds before he nods.

"I think if all the women join forces, it will work; therefore, I think it will be worth trying it again," I confirm as I see the other women nod in agreement.

"What happens with him?" Wulf asks as he inclines his head towards the Keres.

"Once we have a rest, we will try it again, but this time, with all the women," I say as I lean my head back against Caelius's shoulder and close my eyes.

"We need to decide what we are going to do if this works. We need a place to put them to see how long this process lasts, if it lasts any time at all," Caelius says as he holds me closer to his chest.

"I'm calling a meeting with all the other chapters; this is something that everyone should be involved in, something that we need everyone's help in accomplishing," Draco states. "If this works with the Keres, we will throw a party where all the chapters are invited. It will then be decided where we will keep them and for how long." At his low-pitched voice, I feel the darkness taking me, feeling the comfort of Caelius's arms around me.

Even though I'm involved in something scary, in something I would have never imagined before, I feel more comfortable and more at peace than I have felt before.

CAELIUS 10

When I saw Alaia lying on the floor unconscious, I was ready to kill, but after two days of recuperating, they have decided to try again. The Keres, who now we know is called James, is calmer but still not an Elemental. The women have been keeping him in a daze and today will try to change him again. Bion and I will be there to make sure they don't overdo it. Even though the others wanted to be there, the women insisted on it only being two of us. I know that the other brothers will be watching in the computer room to make sure their women are fine.

I don't like the idea of Alaia draining herself for a Keres, but if it helps us find a way of helping all Elementals, I can't stop it. Also, Alaia has confessed to me that she has never felt so useful as she does now, like she is doing what she was meant to do. I walk towards the bathroom where my kitten has just come out of the shower, my eyes running up and down her perfect body as she takes the towel and wraps it around herself.

Taking the couple steps necessary to reach her, I place my hands on her hips and pull her against me. "Are you sure you're feeling up to this already?" I ask as I kiss her forehead, her unique fragrance enveloping me in a blanket of seduction. She raises her hand, stroking my cheek, her breasts rubbing against my chest.

"Well, it depends if you have anything on your mind that would change mine," she teases, which has me as hard as steel in seconds. This woman can turn me on like a light in seconds and have me eating out of her hand with a single look. I place my hands under her perfect ass and lift her up. I walk to the sink and set her down while my hands lower down her legs as I lift the towel up.

"Caelius, have we got time for this?" she asks breathlessly as I kiss her neck, her towel falling around her hips. Looking down, I see her pebbled nipples professing to her excitement. Her hand lowers to my jeans, stroking my hardness, before she starts to unbutton them, when there is a banging on the bedroom door.

"Fuck," I grunt in annoyance. Alaia gasps in surprise, hurriedly lifting the towel around her. I'm going to hang whoever is at the door by their toes. The knock comes again, which has me tensing as I lift Alaia off the counter and onto the floor. Turning, I make my way to the bedroom door, closing the bathroom one on my way out. Yanking the door open, I find Nova standing on the other side with a big smile on her face. Ceric is leaning against the back wall, smirking. The asshole probably knows that they interrupted us.

"Are you guys ready?" Well, so much for hanging the person by their toes. I would never harm Nova or any of the women, for that matter.

"Alaia is just getting ready," I say just as the bathroom door opens and Alaia walks out dressed in her jeans and T-shirt. She looks around, and when she finds her boots, she walks to them, picks them up, and then sits on the bed as she starts to put them on. Nova pushes me aside, and then she's walking in.

"Hi, are you feeling up to it?" Nova asks, which has Alaia's head snapping up in surprise, but then she smiles.

"Feeling much better," she says, and then looks over Nova's shoulder at me and winks, which instantly has my cock twitching in reaction. "I think today, with everyone's cooperation, it will work."

"I think your persuasion has helped with keeping him calm," I say as I stand, ready to make my way to the cell where James is being held. "Let's go. I'm curious to see if this works."

The four of us make our way towards the cell. Once there, I notice that all the women are already here, and so are Bjarni, Draco, Bion, and Celmund. James is sitting on the floor of the cell, his back against the stone wall, a frown on his face. "We will be watching," Celmund says as he leans down and kisses Talia before he makes his way out.

Bjarni hugs Gabriela close to him and says something in her ear before he also leaves. Draco looks around and then at James. I don't know what he's thinking, but his muscles are tense and his features are set. From all the men at the compound, he's the one who oozes danger with a simple glance. "Thank you for doing this. If this works, it will be a breakthrough for all Elementals," he says before he also turns and leaves.

Alaia starts to walk towards the others, but I hold her back. "If you start feeling drained again, I want you to stop, or I'm going to stop it." I see her raise her brows in surprise, but I want her to know that I'm not playing around. Her health comes first. If there is any chance of this hurting her in any way, then I will stop it.

"It will be fine," she murmurs.

"I mean it, Alaia," I state firmly so that she knows I'm serious.

She turns towards me fully and looks up into my eyes. "I know you are, and I will stop if it gets too much." She lifts on her tiptoes and kisses me on the lips before she pulls away and joins the others.

"They're all so damn stubborn," Bion says as he joins me, "but that's why they're our mates." With those words, he bumps his shoulder against mine in comradery. Alaia sits on the floor cross-legged, her hands flat on the ground before her. Brielle sits behind her with her hands flat against Alaia's back. Then all the other women sit in a circle around them. Some are touching Alaia, and others are touching Brielle in one way or another.

"It still surprises me how they use their energy with each other," I state as I see the women close their eyes. I look over at James and see his worried look as he stares at the women.

"What the fuck are they up to?" he asks as he looks over at us.

"They're toasting your ass," Bion grunts, which has the Keres more worried than before.

"What the . . ." His eyes are wide with surprise. He sits like that for a few minutes before they close, and he slumps forward. I look back at the women and see that they all look serene, no distress on any of their faces. The women have always joined forces when working towards something, but from what Alaia was saying last night after meeting with the others, it seems like they are going to try to change that and make the person who is driving what they're doing the conduit.

From what they have been practicing, it seems like when the women are touched by the others, their energy enhances. They become beams of what their gift is. "Do you think he's dead?" Bion asks as he looks into the cell.

I look at James and try to detect his heartbeat but can't from the way he's slumping forward. "If he is, I'm sure they would know," I state, looking at the women again and seeing no change in any of their expressions. Bion and I stand vigilant for the next half hour before the women start to open their eyes. I notice that none of them pull away or stand but sit quietly until Brielle and Alaia have opened their eyes.

James is still in the same slumped position. "It worked," Aria says with a smile as she stands.

"We were able to change him back, but now we need to see how long it will last," Gabriela says as she places her hands flat on the ground behind her and stretches her back.

"If we can find their mates, they should be fine. I saw a woman of about thirty with short black hair when we were healing him, and I think she might be his mate." At Jasmine's comment, the others excitedly start to discuss what they can do next. I make my way towards Alaia, who is still sitting on the ground. Placing my hands under her arms, I lift her up until she's on her feet and her back is against my front. My arm moves around her waist, holding her close to me.

"How are you feeling?" I ask, but suspect she's fine today going by the smile on her face.

"Doing much better than last time, and it worked." At her excited reply, I smile, knowing how nervous she was that it wouldn't work.

"You can open the cell now, and when he awakens, we can see what to do next," Talia says as she walks towards the bars in the cell.

"I don't think that is going to happen yet," Bion states with a frown. At the women's protests, he lifts his hand to try to calm everyone. "We still don't know how long this remedy will last or if he will be completely healed." At his words, I frown. How are we going to keep the women away from James? It might take a long time to find his mate. What if he starts turning again? Elementals are ferocious when turning. Their energy is unpredictable.

"We are going to have to sit with him for a few days until we're sure he's okay," Brielle says, her chin jutting up in confrontation. I see Bion shaking his head before she even finishes her sentence. I'm sure he has the same concerns I do. "Don't shake your head at me,

Bion. You know we have to try to see if we can heal him.”

“We can take turns sitting with him,” Aria says as she walks next to Brielle. “Two of us can sit, maybe for two hours at a time.”

“Why don’t you let us sit with him? You have all already done your bit,” I try to convince them.

“That won’t work,” Scarlett argues.

“Of course not,” Talia confirms. “He’s going to need attention, and more healing maybe. Not to be rude or anything, but you guys wouldn’t know what to do.”

“You’re not sitting with him,” Bjarni says as he walks in, the others close behind.

“Don’t you start, baby. Of course I am,” Gabriela argues.

“It’s way too dangerous,” Wulf grunts as he pulls Jasmine into his arms.

“Why don’t you join us when we are here? If anything happens, then you are here to help,” Talia says with a smirk.

“If he starts to change again, his energy will be unstable,” Burkhart mutters as he pulls Saskia closer to him. “Some elements are controllable, but others, like fire, are hard to contain.”

"Well, if he starts to change, we can always leave, can't we?" Alaia asks as she looks at me. I really want to say no because I would rather her not be anywhere near an Elemental who might change at any moment, but I nod in confirmation. "Well, then, it won't be a problem, as we will feel his rage coming."

"I can take the first two hours," Talia says as she looks at Celmund, who reluctantly nods.

"I'll join you," Nova says, and then looks at Ceric with a raised brow, which has him shrugging in dejection. The women set their schedules, and we reluctantly agree, knowing that if we don't, they will be sitting next to James anyway.

"The party will be arranged for two weeks' time, which should give us enough time to see how he is getting along and if this does work in the long run," Draco says as he walks towards the cell. "Is he stable?" At his question, Bion walks towards the cell door, opens it, and moves inside until he is standing over him. After a quick examination, he reports that James seems to be doing fine.

Everyone starts to leave except for the couples who are going to be sitting for the first two hours. I take hold of Alaia's hand and guide her out of the cell and towards the outside of the compound. "Where are you taking me?" she asks with a laugh.

"You'll see," I say as I guide her towards my favourite place. We walk for a few minutes before the trees open up and the lake appears. I hear Alaia gasp in wonder, and I smile, knowing that she loves it here. I look around and take a deep breath as I see all the wildflowers spread across the ground. There is an eagle flying overhead, but besides that, there is calmness and silence for as far as the eye can see.

"This is so beautiful," Alaia whispers as if she doesn't want to disturb the silence. She lets go of my hand and walks towards a tree to our right. Placing her hand on the tree, she closes her eyes, and then a serene smile lightens her face. I have always found a semblance of peace in this place. I should have known that my woman was one with nature. I brought her here because I knew that it would revitalize her by being around nature. I have realized that she pulls a lot of her energy from her surroundings; therefore, there is nothing more calming or more revitalizing than this place.

ALAIA 11

Today is the day of the party. It has been two weeks since we healed James, and every day we are more assured of our success. He seems to be thriving, and there has been no evidence of any anger. Also, we haven't said anything to him yet, but Celmund believes he has found his mate. If that is true, then our first healing was a huge success.

Today Draco will be talking to the other chapters to discuss the Keres and how we should go about healing them, and then their rehabilitation time. We have noticed with James that there has been no intervention necessary from any of us. After he woke up, he was calm and collected. He did have many questions, and he is filled with regret for the decisions he made while a Keres, but besides that, he has been fine.

Draco has agreed to let James join the festivities, as there will be many Elementals around, so if there is any hint that he might be changing, it will be easy to subdue him. I look back from the mirror and smile to see Sara wiggling into her too-tight black mini dress. She has been quiet the last few days, and I know something is bothering her, but I also know that she won't tell me unless she wants to.

"What do you think?" I ask as I turn in a circle for her to see me. My dress is just as tight as hers. The only difference is that mine is a deep red and the chest area not as low cut as Sara's but still just as provocative. Sara laughs as she looks at me and then winks.

"You look just as good as me," she teases, as we are both wearing our hair down and very little makeup. The only difference between us is the colour of our dresses. "Let's see if that man of yours knows who you are now. I still don't know how he does it," she mutters, which has me laughing.

Sara has been trying to trick Caelius into believing that she is me for the last week, but till now, he has always continued to know who we are, which has just made her try even harder. "He will know, Sara," I say with a chuckle.

"No, he won't. I didn't even let you know what colour your dress was until I brought it in today." Then she frowns and walks towards me suspiciously. "Are you doing something for him to know the difference?" At her question, I shake my head in laughter.

"No, Sara. Trust me, I'm not doing anything." At my confirmation, she nods and then turns around.

"He won't know today, so just keep quiet and follow my lead," she says, which has me shaking my head in amusement and finally agreeing. Caelius has told me that he will never be able to mix us two up, as it is physically impossible for him to be attracted to anyone else besides me. He explained how an Elemental is repulsed by any other woman's touch when they are mated.

I have come to accept the unbelievable. Things I would never have believed before I now accept openly. When Caelius and I shared blood, I was speechless, not knowing what to say or what to do, as I would never have thought that would happen. The natural way with which everyone accepts everyone's differences is amazing. It's as if I'm in an alternative universe where everyone is accepted unconditionally.

Sara has questioned certain things that she has seen, but I have managed to explain them away. I don't know for how long, though, as I hate keeping things from my sister. "Are you ready?" she asks as she slips her feet into her black high-heel pumps. I take the couple steps necessary and also slip into my own red-bottom pumps.

"Ready when you are," I tease, and she walks up to me and slides her arm through mine.

"Let's go and have fun," she says excitedly as we walk out the door. We make it to the courtyard before we encounter Scarlett, Saskia, and Gabriela also walking towards the party.

"Oh wow, look at the two of you," Gabriela says with a whistle. "Today is going to be so much fun. I must warn you, though, that our men never leave our sides when we have parties." Then she points at her kutte and then to Scarlett's and Saskia's. "I see you don't have one of these yet." Then she claps her hands. "This is going to be fun. I think we're going to see Caelius finally lose his composure."

The two women laugh happily at her comment before approaching; they are looking just as beautiful with their party clothes. Scarlett has a tight black strapless blouse with low-cut jeans; Saskia has a long dress with low cleavage and a long slit, and Gabriella has a purple sequin dress that hugs her body in all the right places.

We continue making our way towards the bar area knowing that the party has been extended to outside the compound, as there are six chapters attending the party, most of the men, and apparently they bring women with them too. We can hear the music blaring as soon as we come through the courtyard into the corridor that leads to the bar. When we step into the bar, it's like a different world. There are semi-naked women dancing before the men; some are even kissing or sitting on their laps. I know this is a bikers party, but them being Elementals, I never thought they would celebrate like I've heard the other bikers celebrate.

I look around, seeing all the alcohol imaginable, but one thing I don't see is drugs. Caelius has told me that Draco will not allow drugs within the Elementals MC, but I thought maybe this being a party, there would be. I'm happy to see there isn't.

"Well, hello there, darlings," one guy says happily as he walks up to us. He slots between myself and Sara and places his arms around our shoulders. I see the other three women's look of surprise, and then they are looking around urgently.

"I don't think you should be messing with—" Saskia starts to say, but the man lifts his hand from around Sara's shoulder and tweaks her nose playfully before his hand lands over her shoulder again. I can see her surprised look as she looks across his chest at me and then raises her eyebrow in question.

I take a step forward to try to wiggle out of his embrace, but he brings me back. "Where are you going, darling? Don't be in a hurry," he says happily.

"I'm with someone," I say urgently as I look around, trying to find Caelius. "He won't be too pleased that you're here with me."

"Don't worry, darling, he'll be fine. Two pretty morsels like you are to be shared. He can't be selfish," he says, and then lowers his hand and slaps Sara on the ass, which has her jumping in surprise.

"Listen here, asshole, I'm not one of your toys, okay?" she argues as she pushes at his chest. One minute I'm still trying to step away and the other I see the guy's face snap back as someone punches him. Both Sara and I are pulled away from his falling frame, but his arms are quickly released, and then I see Caelius over the guy.

He says something to the man who is now getting up off the floor, but I can't hear what it is with the noise of the music. I see the man look at us and then back at him. He raises his hands to his chest and shakes his head as he answers. I can see the anger vibrating through Caelius as he steps closer to the man, and my hand goes up to my galloping heart.

Bjarni steps between Caelius and the guy and says something as he places his hands on each man's chest. "My man is so hot," I hear Gabriela say from behind me. I see the other guy say something as if he's apologising, and then Bjarni places his arm around Caelius's tense shoulders and turns him towards me. His eyes clash with mine, and then they travel the length of my body. I can feel myself blush at the heat in his stare.

"How the hell does he do it?" I hear Sara mutter from next to me, but my concentration is on the man approaching me. Before I can say anything, his arms are around my waist and he's pulling me flush against his body.

"You're way too sexy for your own good," he mutters before his mouth crashes down on mine, and we kiss as if there is no one around us. If his arms weren't around me, I would crash to the floor, as my legs have lost all will to stand on their own. My arms lift around his neck, and I kiss him back with all the passion I'm experiencing. I can feel his hardness against my body as I stretch against him.

"Come on!" Sara huffs. "We're surrounded by people and the two of you are acting as if you're alone." I pull away slightly and look into Caelius's eyes; they are such a dark blue at the moment that they look nearly black. His nostrils are flaring in passion as he lifts his head and gently kisses my forehead and then pulls away.

"Do you want something to drink?" he asks, also glancing at Sara to add her to the question. Drink? The only thing I can think about is him, and he's asking me if I want to drink? I nod but don't say anything, as my brain is still trying to catch up to my surroundings.

"Come with me," he says as he takes my hand in his and makes his way towards the bar. I see Kade serving drinks behind the bar, and smile at him. Kade is Scarlett's brother and a great teenager; every time I see him, he has a huge smile on his face. Caelius guides me between the counter and his body, his arms cocooning me between them. He orders our drinks and then looks towards a guy speaking to Sara. "You want me to stop that?" he asks as he inclines his head towards them.

I look at Sara and smile as I see Gunner walking towards her and the unsuspecting guy. "I don't think you will need to," I murmur as I wink. Caelius frowns, but then a look of surprise crosses his face, and he looks at me.

"Gunner and your sister?" he asks.

"There is something there, but I also know that they are avoiding each other for some reason," I say, and see his pensive look as he stretches across the counter to get our drinks. He picks one up and then taps Sara on the shoulder to get her attention and hands it to her. He then gives me mine and his one too. "You want to go see outside?" he asks with a raised brow.

"Sure." I want to see to what extent the Elementals party. I see Nova and Saskia dancing while Burkhart and Ceric stand to one side, looking at them, completely entranced. As we step outside the bar area, I see lanterns spread out throughout the open area of the compound, a big bonfire to one side, and roasting meats on the other side. Again, here we see various men with women draped over them. It seems like the Elementals only have one mate, but they sure enjoy themselves while they look for that one mate.

"Did you also have women like this at the compound? Talia was telling me that Tor has at least eight women living at the club in Cape Town."

At my question, Caelius tenses as he looks around, but then he nods. "Yes, we had a few, but with time, they were asked to leave, as most of the brothers had mates and we didn't really need them here." I can see it's a topic he would rather not be talking to me about, as he looks everywhere except at me, which I find amusing. I look around, dropping the subject, and find Draco standing to one side with a woman next to him trying to get his attention while he speaks to two other men.

I find it amusing how he doesn't even pay attention to how the women fawn around him. I'm sure he's aware of their interest, because I suspect that not much gets past him. "What's Draco's story?" I ask, and Caelius looks over at Draco.

"Well, he's the oldest of all of us," he says, and then shrugs. "He's who maintains the Elementals together. His energy is unmeasured, as it has grown to unfathomable proportions throughout the centuries. He doesn't only bend fire, which is his birth element, but he also bends earth, air, and now I suspect he has started to bend water too. There has never been any Elemental who has been able to do that." His words are full of awe of their leader; I have noticed how close all of them are with each other, which after centuries is understandable, and also how protective they all are of each other.

"Why hasn't he changed if other Elementals with only one century have already changed?" I ask as I look around at everyone.

"He fights it every day. Sometimes we can feel his energy vibrating with the power of his constraint. Once, I asked him, and his answer was that he couldn't leave all of us yet. What worries me is that we all have mates now, and he might think that he can just let go." I can hear the worry in Caelius's voice.

"Would he turn Keres?" That would be a disaster, because with the difficulty we had with James who was only about three centuries old, I can't imagine how it will be with Draco.

"Draco would never allow himself to turn; when he realizes he can't hold it any longer, he will put an end to himself." The anger I feel coming from Caelius has a knot growing in my stomach. I know that it must be heart-wrenching to see someone we love in a position like that.

"Maybe we can continue keeping him calm until he finds his mate; you did say that he knows she's alive."

Caelius looks down at me, a pensive look on his face, but then he shakes his head. "That would be too dangerous. He would drain you," he says as he pulls me against his body.

"But remember, we won't be changing him, only keeping him calm," I say as I place my hand on his chest.

"I will talk to the others and see what they think. I will also speak to Bion and see if he finds that it won't harm you." I know that no matter what, he won't bend when it comes to our safety; therefore, I don't insist but rather make a mental note to speak to the other women and see how we can go about calming Draco.

CAELIUS 12

All the men have been called to a meeting after yesterday's party; I know that Draco has already updated the presidents of the other chapters about what is happening regarding healing of the Keres, and today, they are simply informing all the brothers of what is happening. I don't know yet what they have all decided, but it will be revealed in a few minutes. I see that James is standing close to the front where Draco and Wulf are.

Bjarni and Burkhart have been tasked with keeping an eye on him to make sure he doesn't start to turn without any warning. I was near him a few times yesterday and can vouch for his energy being as calm as any Elemental youngling.

"Everyone, calm down," Wulf calls, which has the men quickly becoming silent.

Draco steps forward, his eyes traveling over all the men present. We, the Elemental MC, have taken the responsibility of keeping our people safe. Maybe now that we have found a way for the Elementals to not turn Keres, our task will simply be to finish off those who resist, and help those who are healed.

"We have good news," Draco says. "As you all know, we have been fighting the Keres for centuries. We think we have now found a way of stopping the change, and if we don't stop it, then we can reverse the process from Keres to Elemental." At his announcement, most of the men start talking. He raises his hand for silence. It takes a minute, but everyone finally settles down.

"I know this is a surprise and unbelievable, but"—Draco points to James—"James was a Keres until two weeks ago. He has been a Keres for the last eighty-six years, but now, as you can see, he has reverted to being an Elemental."

"How is this possible?" one of Tor's men asks as he looks at James suspiciously.

"All I can say is that we can help any of you if you feel like your change is near, and we can also help any Keres change back to being an Elemental except for the ones who have lost their mates," Draco explains. We had agreed at a meeting that the method used to change and help the Keres would be kept secret, as we cannot expose our women.

"We have believed for centuries that once the rage comes on us, we either have to put an end to our lives or change into Keres. Now you are telling us that we have been wrong all along and there actually is a cure," another brother calls out.

"We didn't know about this either until recently. We uncovered some of Vercin's information, and that has led us to believe that this was possible. What we still don't know is how Vercin knew about this."

"So what are we going to do now? Are we going to help those fuckers instead of killing them?" another man asks, which causes a few mutters of revolt. We knew this might happen, as the hate for all the evil that the Keres do is deep. It is hard to help those who have been killing and maiming for sport. Those who have killed our families, killed innocents, but we need to move forward and find a way.

"I would not ask that of you. I know the hate that some have for the Keres, but we need to decide the way forward. When you all get back home, there will be a meeting to discuss the outcome of the Keres in your city. You either vote for us to help them or not. But I must reiterate that we are focusing on the brothers who are feeling a change coming and not so much on the Keres," Draco states.

"How long does this cure last?" one asks.

"We are still investigating. As you can see, James here is as calm as a youngling, but that might change with another Keres. Therefore, we will have to take each one as it comes."

"What happens with the ones who feel like they're about to undergo a change?" one guy standing close to me asks, and I can tell that it's for him, as I can sense his unrestrained energy.

"Talk to Celmund and he will schedule everyone. If you would rather speak to your president, he can also arrange everything," Draco says with conviction, which has the man nodding in acknowledgment. "If any of you suspect another being close to changing, please also let us know, and we will intervene." The conversation continues with men asking questions and Draco answering all of them, and then finally he reveals the last piece that I know will have all the men in a tizzy.

"There is one more thing," he states as he looks around at everyone. "We might also be able to find some of your mates by a method that has been tested recently by some of my men." There is complete silence at this announcement; I can see the scepticism in everyone's faces. "We will only be trying to find the mates of those who are in danger of turning, and as you know, it's not always possible." After that, there is pandemonium, as some of them insist that everyone should get a chance to find their mates before they miss their opportunity.

Draco lifts his hand for attention. This time, it takes a few minutes before they all settle down. "You can discuss it at your meetings, but the method used—it's uncertain if it can find your mates." The men once again ask questions, and the meeting is progressing normally, until one brother decides to mention our women.

"Is this method the women here at the compound? I've heard that they have specific gifts that have no comparison." Instantly, we are all on the alert, as we don't want anyone to know that our women are the methods being used to cure the Keres's rage and play a part in finding our mates. Sooner or later, someone is going to try to approach them, and that we cannot allow.

"The method utilized is of no one's concern at the moment," Draco states with a look at the man that brooks no argument, but it's enough to have the other men curious, and comments start floating about, which has all of us tense and ready to hammer some heads.

If any of these men even think to go speak to any of our women, they will be limping home. I do not want Alaia to overwork herself with this healing even though she claims that it gives her a purpose. Yesterday, when I saw that asshole with his arm around my woman, I was ready to pull his arm out of his body just for touching her. I never thought myself to be possessive, but with Alaia, I'm finding that I don't like men to look at her, much less touch her.

I'm not unreasonable and understand that she's a beautiful woman so there will always be men looking at her. I will curb my anger, as she is mine, and I know that she feels our connection just as deeply as I feel it. Today, I want to give her my stone. I know she hasn't been with me for that long, but her being one with the earth, I know she's ready to have it. Our stones, one for me and one for my mate, are forged when we are born. They are usually identical and protect us against other energies.

Yesterday at the party, I also realized that I haven't gotten her a kutte yet. I need to remedy that as soon as we are done here. I want everyone to know who she belongs to; I want to see my name stretched across her back just like my tattoo is engraved in her skin for all eternity. Yesterday, when I took her back to our room after the party and I had my hands all over her body, caressing her like she deserves, kissing every inch of her scrumptious body, I realised how lucky I am to have found my mate and that she has accepted me with all my scars.

I want her to be able to help the other Elementals, but I saw how exhausted she was after helping James. I'm going to have to discuss this with Draco. We need to make sure that the women aren't going to be overextended with trying to help everyone. I see Burkhart suddenly turn from where he's standing, and by his expression, I know there will be trouble. He has never been one to be very patient, and it doesn't look like he's going to start today.

I make my way towards where he is, his muscles tense as he looks at another brother who is talking to two others. "You must try," Burkhart says, which has Rex, the brother from our chapter in Johannesburg who was talking, snap around to look at him.

"Why would only some be privileged? If your women can help us, then they have the obligation to help us all," Rex says angrily as he takes a step towards Burkhart. Not being one to step down, he's about to approach Rex, when I place a hand on his shoulder.

"Let's resolve this later; we will take Rex aside and explain to him how things work," I mutter, hoping that Burkhart will listen to me. We don't want to make a big thing of this or the other brothers will pick up on the fact that maybe our women are responsible for what is happening, and then we will have a fight on our hands when more of them insist on talking to them.

Burkhart looks over his shoulder at me furiously and is about to talk, when he picks up on what I'm trying to tell him. I see him take a deep breath. "Motherfucker," he mutters before he turns and walks back towards where he was next to James. I don't look back but take the steps required to reach Rex, glad to notice that not many brothers noticed the exchange, as they are all listening to Draco's suggestions of the way forward.

"What?" Rex asks angrily as he looks at me. "If they can help us, then you should let them help all of us."

"Remember, Rex, before you start insisting that they do whatever you are thinking, they are our women. As such, we protect what is ours; Draco has answered the question about the method to this treatment. Now you can both listen to him and bid your time while we work on this new system, or you can answer to us if you try anything with any of our women," I threaten.

I see his muscles are tense and that he is contemplating taking a swing at me. I'm actually hoping that he does because his arrogance is starting to piss me off. "He's just disappointed to know that there might be a chance to find our mates but we might not be able to get that chance," one of the other brothers from the Johannesburg chapter intervenes as he slaps Rex lightly on the back.

"We are still investigating other opportunities, but as you know, not everyone has mates alive yet; therefore, this becomes a mute topic, as we have to try to help those who might be on the verge of changing first." At my reply, the men around us nod in agreement. Even Rex huffs and lifts his hands in surrender. This situation has been handled, but how many other men out here believe the same as what Rex believes? Are we going to have problems trying to keep our women safe because of what they can do? Did we make it worse? Instead of only fearing the Keres trying to capture our women, now we might have to fear our brothers wanting to get close to them too.

The meeting ended a couple minutes later, and all the brothers prepared to leave. Draco asked that the other presidents come back with their decisions so that we can start to prepare. All the responses need to be in by the end of next week, and then the work truly begins.

ALAIA 13

It has been an intense week since the party; we have had an Elemental from the Cape Town chapter come in who has been struggling not to turn. At first, we started to heal him as we did the Keres but soon realized that with him, it was different. Instead of surrounding him with love, we had to try to calm him. Therefore, we realized that we might encounter this problem with each different person we try to heal. We changed around, and Brielle took control, as she has a unique way of calming people.

We were also able to see his mate, and this time, Gabriela was able to pinpoint a location, which helped the men find her. After James's and the Elemental's mates were found, we have hope that we might be able to find more mates. We have also sat down and discussed Draco, and we think we might be able to calm him from afar if the men don't agree to us trying to help him, even though seeing as this whole process works, we are certain he will start to feel the interference with his energy as soon as we start.

Today we have decided to try. As soon as the kids are down for a nap, we are going to get together and try to see what we can do for him. I just need to see where he is so that I can direct all our energy through the earth to him. I look towards Brielle, who is twisting her hands in nervousness while we wait for Jasmine, Aria, and Gabriela to still join the rest of us.

"What's wrong?" I ask, and see her startled look, as her thoughts seemed to be far away.

"It's just that this is Draco," she explains as she shrugs. "His energy is incomparable. We need to be strong to calm him. Also, he doesn't know anything about this. What if he's not pleased?"

"We are trying to help the man. I'm sure he will be fine as soon as he starts feeling our mojo entering his sexy body," Nova teases with a wink. "We will just have to make sure that the calmness has him nice and chilled before he can get to us."

"This isn't funny, Nova. He might get upset with the guys, thinking that they asked us to do this," Brielle states.

"You're stressing way too much. He might get upset, but he will understand that we just want to help him. Also, we're going to try to find his mate. What else could a guy ask for?" Nova says in a more serious tone.

"Well, let's hope you're right," Brielle says just as the others join us.

"Let's start. Draco is in the computer room, but I'm not sure how long he will stay there," Talia says as she looks at her phone.

"We can sit right here, then. I can reach him from here," I state as I look around at the courtyard. Brielle looks around and then sits down under the beautiful tree situated in the middle of the courtyard. I sit next to her and place my hands on the ground. Brielle places one of hers on top of mine, and then all the others sit around us and touch us in one way or another. I close my eyes and start feeling the energy beneath my fingertips. Soon, I feel Brielle's warmth stroke over my skin, and then its flowing through me.

I direct the healing force through the ground until it's in the computer room, and then I feel for the strongest energy. I find it immediately. I knew Draco was powerful, but this is beyond anything I thought capable. I know that the others can feel the same that I am feeling and will know the strength of his power.

The women's energy surrounds me with its power, growing to try to match Draco's. I am surprised at the strength that I feel flowing through me. The calmness Brielle is sending, together with the energy of love that I am directing towards him, should have him as mellow as a baby in no time. I feel a disturbance in the flow and know that he is moving. I follow his movement but don't break the connection. We continue with the healing until we all start to feel a draining. I stop the flow of energy and take a deep breath before I open my eyes.

I gasp when I see Draco standing a few meters away with his arms crossed over his chest. The other men are surrounding us. Their expressions vary as they patiently wait for us to open our eyes. I can't tell if Draco is upset or not, as his expression is bland. My eyes snap around until I find Caelius. His hands are in his back pockets as he stands relaxed, looking at us.

The women retrieve their hands but sit quietly, waiting for Draco. I'm hoping he sees that we were trying to help him. It's amazing how he is standing there as if nothing happened. The other Elemental was sleeping by the time we finished with the healing. Draco is standing there as if nothing has perturbed his energy.

"Did you all have fun?" he asks with a raised brow.

"We were just trying to help," Scarlett says. "We thought that maybe we could find your mate, same way as we found the previous two."

"Don't be upset with the guys. They didn't know anything about this," Aria says quickly, which has Brandr shaking his head in exasperation.

"Oh, I know that. My men would never be foolish enough to try to poke my energy," he states.

"Did it work?" Nova asks as she inclines her head. "It will be really disappointing if we managed to poke you and then nothing." At her teasing words, I bite my lip, trying not to laugh. Nova has no idea when to be quiet, which is something that has made me love her for the unique and open person she is.

I hear Ceric groan as he shakes his head in defeat, which has Bion grunting in amusement. "Are you all going to try this again?" Draco asks without answering the question.

I see Gabriela shrug before she speaks. "That depends on you. I don't think it can hurt, and besides, I saw your mate." At her comment, I see Draco and all the men, tense waiting for Gabriela to continue, but she simply sits there smiling at them. These women are truly fabulous. With all these dangerous men standing before us, anyone would have thought we would cower, but no, we sit here teasing them.

"Just get it out already, baby girl," Bjarni growls impatiently.

"Don't you go talking to me in that tone, you lug, or you won't hear it today." At her comment, I can't help it. I throw back my head and laugh, which has the others soon joining in. By the time we start to quieten, I realize that the men were also laughing, and that Draco is standing there shaking his head with a smile on his face. Gosh, that man has killer dimples. Whomever his mate is, she will be fighting the women off him at every turn; I hope she's feisty, because with Draco, I think she will have to be.

"Well, would you like to know what I saw?"

Draco doesn't say anything but just lifts his eyebrow.

"Oh, you're no fun," Gabriela says playfully. "Okay, well, the good news is that she's closer than you think. And, Draco, you are going to love her. That woman has hair that rivals the flames." I can see him tense at her words. I can imagine that his curiosity must be driving him, but he won't say anything.

"What do you mean closer? Where is she?" Bjarni asks with a frown.

"She's in town." At my words, the men all look at Draco. At first, there is no indication that he heard me, but then he gives me a slight nod and turns. He is out of the courtyard in the blink of an eye, the men following him. All I hear is someone saying, "Thank fuck," before there is just us again.

"Do you think they will find her?" Jasmine asks with a frown.

"Nope, she will find him," Gabriela says with a laugh.

"What do you mean?" Saskia asks as she stands and stretches her back.

"Katrina, that's her name, appears to have the gift of finding things," Gabriela reveals, "and it looks like she is looking for her man."

Nova claps her hands excitedly. "This is so cool. Are you telling me that you sent all the men on a wild goose chase?"

"Well, they did seem like they needed the fresh air, and I was getting tired of having their inquiring eyes on us," Gabriela says innocently, which has all of us laughing.

"These poor guys don't know what has hit them when you all band together," I say teasingly.

"You are now a part of us too, Alaia. It's not when you all band together but when we all band together," Jasmine says as she also stands. I see the others nod in agreement as they also start to stand. I believe they have taken me in as one of them because I feel a connection with these women that I have never felt before with anyone except Sara.

Talking about Sara, I wonder how it's going today. Gunner went out into town to get some items that we needed at the compound, and Sara was invited to tag along. It seems that whatever was keeping them apart has now gone, because I can see the look on their faces when they look at each other. There is something going on with those two.

I have also asked Sara to look at what is happening with Joshua and if he is okay. She tells me that he is fine, which pleases me in a way, but breaks my heart in another way, as he won't answer my calls. I know he doesn't understand how I could have chosen to stay here instead of leaving with him, but I'm hoping with time, he will realize that I'm happy, and he will forgive me. Caelius has asked if I want him to go speak to Joshua and try to show him that he has good intentions, but I refused, as I doubt Joshua will listen at the moment.

"Well, now that we have done our good deed for the day, what should we get up to?" Saskia asks with a smirk.

"You are up to no good, Saskia," Nova says with a clap. "I love it. Spill the beans."

"Well, I was thinking that it's such a lovely day outside and the men are too busy searching for a woman they apparently aren't going to find today, so why don't we go down to the lake for a swim?" I love the suggestion, but I don't have anything to swim with. My mind races over what underwear I have that I might be able to use.

"That's perfect. I've only used my bikini once, and that ended quite well, I'll let you know," Jasmine quips with a huge smile.

"Well, if everyone is in agreement, we can meet at the lake in the next half hour?" Scarlett asks as she prepares to leave. The women start to disperse, and I am nearly at our room when Talia stops me.

"Alaia, have you managed to get any swimwear yet?" I'm surprised she realized that I might not have anything to wear. I shake my head and then shrug.

"No, but I will just wear my underwear."

"Nonsense. I have extra, unless you don't want to wear my stuff," she says.

"Oh, I don't have a problem with wearing any of your stuff," I quickly assure her, as I don't want her to think I'm ungrateful. "If you're sure, it will be great."

I find myself wearing a sexy red bikini as I pull off my T-shirt and place a towel on the ground. Saskia was right;

the day is nice and warm and perfect for lazing around next to the lake.

Brielle yelps as she starts to enter the water. "This water is freezing cold," she complains as she starts to splash her body with water to get used to the temperature.

I smirk as I remember a trick I used to pull with Sara when I was a kid. I walk close to the water and get my feet in until they are ankle deep. A few minutes later, I have heated the water enough for it not to feel uncomfortable. "Brielle, do you want to come over here and see something?" I ask, and she readily approaches. When she's about five steps away from me, she stops, and then a radiant smile lights her face.

"How did you do it?" she asks as she claps in happiness.

"I peed in the water," I say seriously, which has her smile slip for a second before she throws back her head and laughs.

"You must have been holding it for a month if you were able to warm up all this water." We both start to laugh at our own jokes.

"What's so funny?" Scarlett asks as she places her foot in the water and then steps back with a scowl.

"Come over here," I call, and she walks towards us but keeps out of the water. "Come on in. Don't be chicken." At that, she shakes her head.

"I don't really like cold water," she mutters. "You want me in a bad mood, make me a bath or a shower with cold water."

"It's warmer here," Brielle says with a laugh.

"Yeah, I doubt it can be much warmer than over there." But she still puts her foot forward and lightly places it in the water. After a minute, it's right up to her ankle. "How is this possible? It's a couple degrees warmer than over there."

Brielle knocks her hip against mine and then inclines her head towards me. "We have our own water heater over here." The women and children loved the idea of the warmer water. We spent most of the afternoon frolicking in the water and laughing at each other's comments. The sun was high in the sky when we first saw Wulf and Caelius coming through the cropping of trees, their T-shirts moulding to their muscles, professing to their perfect bodies.

CAELIUS 14

Celmund told us that the women were down by the lake. What he forgot to tell us was that they were all swimming. The others are just behind us, and I can imagine that their reaction will be the same as mine. The thought of any man seeing my woman like that doesn't sit well with me, but I know I can't stop her from doing the things that are normal to them.

"Fuck," I hear Wulf grunt, his face a mask of annoyance.

"I feel you, Brother, but you know we can't stop them from doing all the things they love doing, or this will become a prison for them," I state, and I know Wulf understands what I'm saying, as he nods his head.

"We're all mated except for Draco, and I doubt he will be coming down here," Wulf says, which has me smiling, as I had already thought the same thing. All the brothers are mated, so there is no chance of them ogling another woman.

I see Alaia look up and see me. A radiant smile appears on her face. I'm trying to keep my eyes on her face, as I know that if my eyes travel down her body again, I will be carrying her to our room and we won't come out for dinner. Orion starts to run when he sees his father, his little arms waving in the air in excitement. I see the smile of love on Wulf's face as he kneels and opens his arms to await his son.

I wonder when I will be doing the same thing. I have always wanted children and a mate. The thought of my kitten swollen with my child has my good intentions lost as I look over her body in her red bikini. Her perfect breasts are straining against the cups of her bikini, her tapered waist swelling out to her luscious hips. I see Orion jump the last step into his dad's arms, and Wulf stands and throws him up in the air as I step closer to Alaia.

I place my hands on her hips and pull her against me. Her arms lift, and she places them around my neck. "I missed you," she murmurs before my mouth crashes down on hers. I shouldn't be doing this, as I'm already hard. Her body so close to mine, rubbing up and down against me, is going to have me ready to burst if I don't be careful.

I lift my head after giving her a thorough kiss and take a step back. "Have you had fun today?" I ask, and her eyes light up with joy.

"She's our personal heater," Gabriela says as she pulls the twins out of a water puddle where they're playing. I look at her and then at Alaia again, wondering what they are talking about.

"What's this about a personal heater?" I ask, and she blushes.

"Since I was a kid, I've been able to heat the water in specific places because it's part of nature." She inclines her head towards the water. "The water here is really cold, so I kind of heated a portion of it so whoever wanted to swim could."

I smile as I shake my head; this woman never ceases to surprise me. "You are hot," I murmur, which makes Aria, who is standing behind me, snicker.

"Oh boy, here they come," Saskia says as she picks up her towel and wraps it around her body. I find myself grinning as I look over my shoulder and see the others' perplexed faces when they see their women in their bikinis.

"I'm going into the water," Brielle says as she hurriedly makes her way there.

"I'm coming with," Scarlett says, and hurries after her.

"Chicken," Nova quips, but joins them with a wide smile on her face. At this, I laugh as I see her pregnant belly displayed for all to see.

"Baby girl, wha—" Bjarni starts, but Gabriela stops his tirade as she jumps into his arms and kisses him.

"What the hell are you doing now, hellcat?" Ceric grunts as he walks towards the water's edge. I see Nova shrug with an innocent look on her face.

"Whatever do you mean? I'm enjoying the perfect day," she says demurely.

"Come on out of the water, hellcat. Let's go to the compound. I got you marshmallows." At Ceric's persuasive words, she takes a step towards him and then stops. Nova has been craving marshmallows, and today, Ceric made sure to go into a store and get her the biggest bag he could find.

"Thank you, hot stuff, but this water is so nice," she quips as she kicks her foot and splashes him.

"Nova!" he growls. "You're not even enjoying the water, woman. Only your feet to your knees are in the water." With those words, he steps into the water and towards her, which has her squealing and trying to rush the other way, but of course, Ceric is on her before she can even take another step. She laughs happily as he pulls her into his arms and starts walking out of the water. "You're going to be the death of me," he mutters, which has Scarlett and Brielle laughing.

"No, I won't. You don't die, remember?" she teases. I see that the others have also reached their women, and it seems like all of them are losing the fight against them, except for Burkhart, who is already striding up the path with Saskia in his arms.

"Do you want to go in for a swim?" Alaia asks as she places her hand on my chest.

"I don't have anything to swim in."

"You can go in your boxers," she says. "I can even warm the water if it's too cold for you." I know what she's trying to do, and if she wants it, then I'm willing to please her. I pull off my T-shirt and then slide my jeans down my legs. I see Alaia's smiling face and the passion filling her eyes as she looks at my body. I hear a gasp from behind me and only now remember that I took my T-shirt off before the women.

Some of them have never seen my scars; Alaia takes my hand and pulls me towards the water. I follow her until we are at the water's edge, and then I lean down and throw her over my shoulder, which has her yelping in surprise. "What are you doing?" she asks in a laugh as she starts to kick her legs.

I lightly slap her perfect ass, which has her gasping. "Did you just slap my bum?" I slap it again. "You're incorrigible, you rebel."

"You wanted to go into the water. Well, kitten, we are going into the water," I tease. When I get to waist-high, I slide her off my shoulder and into my arms. Her eyes are shining in happiness, and then I lower her slowly until her bum touches the water.

"Ohhh, that's cold," she gasps as she tries to slide up my body, making me laugh. I see her foot move, and I know she's going to try to warm the water, so I pull her up again until she's dangling in a way where she isn't able to touch the water. "Caelius, don't you dare," she gasps just before I lower her again, and this time, the water circles her midriff before I pull her up.

She slaps me on the shoulder with her hand. "It's cold," she gasps.

"I don't think so. I thought you wanted me to swim with you?" I tease, and she scowls at me.

"I've changed my mind. You are mean," she mutters as she looks over her shoulder at the water, which has me throwing my head back and roaring with laughter. I let her legs slightly down so that her feet can touch the water, knowing that she will start to warm the water, and wait. Soon, I start to feel the temperature of the water warming. It's amazing how she can warm this expanse of water at the speed she is.

"Shall I let you down now?" I ask, and I'm awarded a smile and a nod. I let her slide down my body, her wet body stroking my skin, igniting my passion to a fever pitch. When her feet are touching the bottom of the lake, I lower my head and kiss her gently before lifting her again. "Place your feet over mine. There are sharp stones that might hurt you."

She smiles up at me and then instead of placing her feet over mine, she jumps up and folds her legs around my waist, which has my hardness cradled against her heat. "I think you could heat up the water with that thing alone," she murmurs against my neck as she nips it. I smile as my cock twitches against her, confirming my arousal.

I look over my shoulder and see that most of the couples have already left. Only Bion, Brielle, Cassius, and Scarlett are still around, but they are also packing to leave. I move my hand down over my woman's bum and move her slightly against me, making us both groan. Her hand slides down my chest and over my cock, and she rubs it just right that has me wanting to plunge deep into her.

"Pull my boxers down, kitten." My voice is low and raspy as I fight against the urge to take her fast. She brings the other hand down and does as I ask. My cock jumps out into her hand. I take hold of the bikini bottoms and pull them to the side. Lifting her slightly, I mutter, "Put him in," and groan as I feel him slide through her folds until he is sliding deep into her.

"Oh," Alaia gasps, and then pulls her hands around my neck. I walk deeper into the lake, wanting to make sure that no one realizes what we are doing, and I don't want my brothers to hear my woman. As I walk, the motion makes Alaia dig her nails into my shoulders in pleasure. We move until the water is up to Alaia's shoulders and by my chest. I place both my hands on her bum and start to move her up and down my hardness, the motion intensifying our passion.

I take her mouth, kissing her with everything I have, her movements jerky as I feel her muscles tightening around me. She groans as she clamps down around me. With her release, I don't hold back any longer as my climax explodes. We stand here holding each other as our breathing calms.

"You're going to kill me one of these days." I grunt in amusement at her words and feel her nip my neck in response.

"Caelius," I hear Bion's tone of warning, which has me tense and ready for a fight in a second. I look over my shoulder at him and see him incline his head towards the south. I look towards the south and see movement by the wall that joins our property to a nature reserve and the road. I pull out of Alaia and fix her bikini bottoms.

"Pull up my boxers, kitten," I say as I start to make my way towards where Bion and Cassius are standing, their women standing behind them. Cassius has his phone out and is texting, whom I'm guessing is Celmund.

"What's wrong?" Alaia asks. I can see the worry on her face, and that is something I don't want ever to happen. I don't want my woman to ever be afraid of anything.

"Don't worry, kitten. It's just trespassers we saw coming over our wall. The others will go stop them, but we need to go in and get ready for dinner." I try to appease her, but my body is tense with the thought of them being Keres. I notice that Alaia doesn't ask any more questions or procrastinate. She hurries towards her stuff and is ready to move.

Cassius, Bion, and I place the women before us as we make our way back to the compound. I want to pick up Alaia and rush towards safety, but I don't want to panic the women. We are nearly at the compound when Cassius's phone starts to ring.

"Yeah," he mutters.

"Get in here now," Celmund says, which with our acute hearing, we all hear, and in a second, we have the women in our arms and are sprinting towards the compound garage door where we see Draco and Wulf standing. I can see by Draco's intense look that shit is going down.

"Go inside. Hurry up," Draco says to the women as we make it to the garage. I see Alaia's look of concern, which has my anger rising. I lower my head and kiss her gently before she turns and hurries inside.

"What the fuck is going on?" Cassius asks as we hear the compound shutting down.

"Prepare yourselves. We're going to have other Elemental company." At Wulf's reply, I tense. The motherfuckers are going to try to attack us to get to our women. We are trying to help those assholes, and this is what they do.

"Who?" Bion asks as he opens the compartment where we keep our weapons. I join him in taking my weapons of choice. I always carry a gun at the back of my jeans, but now I place a holster around my legs with two long blades and two more guns.

"Johannesburg Chapter. There are at least six of them," Draco states as he walks outside,

"Does Diesel know this?" Cassius asks as he joins Draco outside. We are all tense, as we don't like a fight near our women, but not only that—we fight Keres. We don't fight each other. Elemental fighting Elemental is not something we ever thought would happen.

"Apparently not. He sent them on a run. I guess they decided this was more important," Wulf grunts.

"Where are the others?" I ask as I go stand next to the others in the room.

"Bjarni, Ceric, and Brandr have gone to the east. Burkhart and Gunner have gone around the back, but you know they will pick them up the same as we would. We will wait here for them. If they want to challenge us, we will accept," Draco states.

"It was that fucking Rex. I thought he had accepted that we would in time update everyone. I should have let Burkhart on him," I state, thinking of the confrontation the other day.

"They're close," Draco says, which has us all spreading out. A few minutes later, we see them coming through the trees, their energy levels ready for a fight.

"Are you sure you want to do this?" Draco asks when they're close enough to hear him.

"We want the opportunity to find our mates. You have no right to keep it to yourself and decide who gets to find them and who doesn't," Sloan, one of the brothers, says. I see that Rex is among them but standing more to the back. I'm sure he was the instigator, but now stands back instead of showing his face as the culprit.

"I didn't have to tell you about it, did I?" Draco asks with a raised brow. "We don't have the facilities at the moment to give everyone a chance. Therefore, we have to give it to the ones who need it the most, and as you know, those are the Elementals who are nearing their change, which from what I can see from here, is none of you."

"You can't know that. We have a right like everyone else," Marcus says this time. "I want to make sure that if my mate is out there, I find her and don't miss her because someone else had the opportunity that I didn't have."

"If the rumours are true, and it is your women who can find our mates and can stop us from turning, then I don't understand what the problem is. I'm sure they're not that delicate that an extra six men will break them." The way the asshole insinuates that has me ready to punch him, but I don't need to worry, because soon, he is gasping for air, his face turning purple.

I look over at Draco because only he is capable of extracting all the air from an area, but he has never done it in the open before. I see that he hasn't moved, professing to his ability and how much his power has grown. When the asshole falls to his knees, finally gasping in big gulps of air, I see the frightened look on the others' faces when they realize how precarious their position is.

"We don't want any trouble. We just want the opportunity to find our mates," Sloan says.

"If you didn't want trouble, you wouldn't have come over the wall, and yes, through the main gate," Cassius says.

"You do know that you went against something that our club president said, don't you?" Bion asks. "For that, there will be consequences."

"Who gives you the right to be judge and jury on something that relates to our lives?" Rex asks angrily.

"Everyone's life is important, every single Elemental. We will not bend on this. We will not look at your case while there are other Elementals out there in precarious positions," Draco states.

"We cannot flick a switch and know where your mates are. It takes investigating and research. We cannot find everyone even if we wanted to," I state, trying to appease the tension between everyone.

"Fuck off, Caelius. Why would we believe you? What are you all getting out of this? I'm sure there must be something if you are only willing to choose those in desperate need. Do you require them to pay you once they come here? Because if that's what it takes, we can also pay." At Marcus's comment, I know they have gone too far. I can feel everyone's energy levels rise.

Fighting Elementals will not be the same as fighting Keres because their energy is still pure and stronger. I see one of them raise his arm and know that even if we didn't want this, we are going to have to show them that this is not acceptable.

A ball of flame is suddenly flying towards us; the motherfucker thinks he can use these simple tricks on us. I lift my arms and send a gust of wind that disperses the flame and finally blows it out, but already there are more flying towards us. Draco lifts his hands, and a wall of flame appears between us and the others. The balls of flame disperse within the heat of the wall.

I hear a rush of water and know that one of them must be a water bender trying to kill the flames of Draco's wall of fire. I look over at Bion and see him smile as he lifts his hands and rotates them anti-clockwise. I see the rush of water that was moving towards us suddenly turn and move towards the others. It's not easy to mess with a brother's bending, so for Bion to be able to stop the momentum of the rush of water and bend it to his will shows the strength of his power.

Wulf goes down on his haunches and places his hands on the ground. By the force of the energy, I can tell that Ceric and Bjarni are bending too. I can feel the earth starting to move and bend, and then wide cracks open towards where the Elementals are. I see them rush in different directions, exactly what we were expecting. Now we can hunt them down individually instead of them being together, pulling from each other's powers.

I automatically turn to my left and take off after one of them rushing that way, knowing that my brothers will follow the others. My senses are alert; as I run, I lift my arms and start to bend the air in the direction this particular Elemental is going. The wind will carry back his scent and let me know where the asshole is heading. I know he has stopped when I feel heat come towards me; my anger intensifies as I realize the son of a bitch is bending fire in the middle of a forest where everything will go up in flames. Contrary to Draco, I cannot extract air. The only thing I can do is try to guide the flames so they don't burn our home.

I see a flash of fire moving towards me. I send a flash of air to guide the fire until it's hitting the ground a few metres before me. I pinpoint the asshole's location. Lifting my gun, I aim and then shoot. A minute later, I hear a grunt. Before he has a chance to move, I rush towards him. I jump at the last minute onto his back as he tries to get away.

"Son of a bitch," I grunt before I pull back my fist and punch him. He manages to lift his leg and knee me in the side. I grunt as I roll out of his way and onto my feet. He also stands. "Is this really what you want?" I grunt as I lift my leg and kick his knee, making him go down again.

"Yes, you can't tell us who does and who doesn't have the right to find their mate," he grunts. I pull back my arm and punch him again.

"We would let everyone find their mates if we could, but it doesn't work that way. Stop being an ass." He charges at me, his head butting me in the stomach, which has the air leaving my lungs. As I stagger back, I pull out one of my blades.

"Don't make me do this, Brother," I grunt, but the son of a bitch just smiles at me and lifts his gun. Before I can think, I throw my blade, hitting him right where his heart is. Instantly, he starts to disintegrate into a white-hot flame before it turns to ashes and blows away. I lower my head in anger. Why would he do this? Why would any of them do this? I just killed an Elemental unnecessarily because they were selfish and weren't thinking of anyone except themselves.

ALAIA 15

I don't know what the threat might be, but I'm worried it could be Joshua. Is Joshua doing something he shouldn't? Did he bring more guys with him this time? After being with the Elementals for a while, I know there is no chance of a group of marines being able to win a fight with them. I asked Sara to see how Joshua is doing and am now waiting for her to update me on where he is.

Some of the women have gone into the computer room to see what is happening. The others are here with us in the kitchen, keeping themselves busy so as not to think of what might be happening outside. The thought of Caelius being hurt has my heart racing in anguish. I need to know he's fine. I stand from the table and walk towards the stone wall of the kitchen; placing my hand there, I close my eyes and let my senses take me through the earth to where I can feel him. My stomach knots when I feel the anguish he is feeling. Did something happen? Is one of the guys hurt?

I'm pleased to know he is fine, but why would he be feeling so anguished? I see Saskia looking at me with a questioning look, and I shrug. "Just wanted to see if Caelius is fine. He is," I say, not elaborating, as I don't want to worry anyone.

"This is terrible. I have always hated it when the men have a fight," Brielle says as she raises her hand in frustration. "Maybe once we stop the men from turning, we will be able to end this Keres epidemic that has the men constantly in danger."

I hope she's right, because from what I have seen, the Keres are evil, and if they have the opportunity, they will kill any of us. After James's change and the conversations we have had with him since then to try to understand the Keres better, we have come to realize that the fury takes over their whole mind and body, completely overpowering their good side.

James and his mate have been joined. At first, we were worried that because he had already changed before that, the bonding wouldn't work like it does with the Elementals, that maybe somehow they wouldn't have the same magnetism, but to our delight, it seems like they are as compatible as any Elemental.

James has been moved to one of the Elementals' chapter compounds that is out of the way so that he can be monitored in case something changes or goes wrong. There have been many requests from the different chapters for help with some of their men. Celmund has been booking them in, insisting on only booking one a day even though we have confirmed that we can help at least two a day, but the men are adamant that they don't want us to tire ourselves.

I know that if they could, they would only let us do one a week, but they know that there are too many for them to deny them the opportunity of getting better. I heard Celmund telling Wulf that he is finding it difficult to prioritize, as there are quite a few who are precarious. The thought that there are so many men who have gone through their very long lives looking for that one person who fulfils them completely and fully to the extent that their dark side never comes out is sad.

"It will take a long time before the Keres come to an end, because as many Elementals as there are, there are more Keres," Saskia says as she opens a packet of crisps and starts to nibble on them. "I just hope that fool man of mine doesn't do something stupid and get himself killed."

Out of all the men, we all know Burkhart is a hothead and explodes at the least provocation. Therefore, Saskia's fears are well-founded.

"Yes, he does have a hothead, but you know that man of yours isn't easy to kill," Brielle says as she walks towards Saskia and hugs her from behind.

"Do you think there is anything we can do to help them?" Nova asks as she stuffs another marshmallow into her mouth.

"No, I don't think so, as we don't even know who they're fighting," Brielle says with a frown.

"If Ceric gets hurt, I swear he will be sorry," Nova mutters under her breath, which has me smiling as I imagine all the things she will come up with to torture the poor man.

"If he knows what's good for him, he will start running the other way now," Scarlett says playfully, which has Nova sticking her tongue out at her.

"I will just have to run after him." At that, we all burst out laughing when we imagine Nova with her swollen belly running after Ceric as she argues with him. "What? You think I wouldn't?" she quips with a raised brow, and then also laughs. Just then, Talia walks in, a tense look on her face.

"What's happening?" Brielle asks as soon as she sees her.

"It's Elementals from the Johannesburg Chapter; they wanted to corner Draco into letting them find their mates. Needless to say, they just started fighting. I couldn't stand the suspense. I had to leave." Just then, we feel the earth moving beneath us, which has me gasping.

"What the hell is happening out there?" Nova mutters as she places her hand over her stomach.

"Draco must be furious. He's trying to help the Elementals, and then you have them come here to throw it back in his face," Saskia says as she shakes her head sadly.

"You have no idea; he was suffocating one of the guys without even batting an eye. From Celmund's excited reaction—" She looks at our surprised looks. "Yes, excited, as apparently he has never seen anyone extract oxygen as easily as Draco was doing, especially outside in the open."

"That man has some powers on him," Brielle says. "Did you feel his energy when we were trying to calm him?"

"I think his pinkie has more compressed energy than an atomic bomb," Talia states. "The ease with which he bends the elements is crazy."

"What do you mean bends the elements?" We all snap around at Sara's question. We were so distracted that we didn't even see her walk in. By her shocked look, I can tell that she heard more than we wanted her to hear. I should have already said something to her, as she will now feel like I am betraying her by not trusting her with this secret, but it's not my secret to tell. "Is anyone going to tell me what you are talking about?"

"You know how we all have gifts," I say, and wait for her nod. "Well, Draco also has a gift. He can bend the elements." At my confession, I see her eyes widen, and then she looks around at the other women before looking back at me.

"All the elements?" she asks.

"I'm not sure, but fire, air, and earth he can bend," I state.

"Are you kidding me?" she asks, and has us all shaking our heads in reply.

"How long have you known about him?" I knew this question was coming. I know Sara is going to be hurt by my omission.

"From the beginning," I confirm, and instantly her face shuts down. "It wasn't my place to say anything." I try to justify my actions, but I know she won't see it as such.

"You can tell me about all the women having gifts, but you can't tell me that Draco does?" I see her frown, and then she asks what I was hoping she wouldn't. "Do the other men have gifts too?" At her question, I see the others look at me. I don't know what to do. How am I going to explain that all the men bend the elements.

"Yes," I state, which has her gasping in surprise. Her hand raises to her chest, and she looks at the others. "What do they do?"

"They all bend the elements," I state before anyone else can say anything.

"All of them do the same thing?" she asks suspiciously.

"Not the same as Draco. They usually only bend one element."

At my admission, she looks at me with hurt in her eyes. "You didn't trust me to tell me," she states before she shakes her head and turns to leave.

"Sara," I call. She stops but doesn't turn back to me. "I couldn't tell you. It wasn't my place to say anything." She doesn't say anything as she walks out. I want to run after her and try to make up for it, but the truth is that I didn't tell her and she has every right to be upset. Up till now, we have always told each other everything and not had secrets with each other. I know this will feel like a betrayal, and she has every right to feel like that, as I don't have an excuse for what I did except that I was trying to protect something that no one knows about, and if they did, there would be a riot.

"I'm sorry, sweetheart," Brielle says as she looks at me. I give her a small smile, but my heart is hurting for having hurt Sara. I don't like being upset with anyone, especially not Sara, as we have always been very close. I now feel like I have betrayed her, because in a way, I have by not letting her know.

"Excuse me," I call out as I follow Sara. I need to make her understand. I walk out of the kitchen and start to turn towards where Sara has her room, when I see her sitting under the tree in the courtyard. I know that she knows I am approaching her, but she is purposefully ignoring me. When I am standing before her, I can see that she has tears running down her cheeks, and that tears at me like a knife knowing that I am responsible for her tears.

"I'm sorry," I say, but she doesn't acknowledge me. "I couldn't tell you as it's their secret. Also, I wanted to keep you safe for as long as I could, because knowing they have this gift could be dangerous." I try to think of the right words to explain my decision at the time not to say anything. "You haven't seen Caelius's back, but it is scared badly from a group of vampire hunters who thought that because they are different, they need to be ended." At my confession, I see her eyes widen in surprise.

"You know that I would never have said anything," she mutters.

"Not even if you thought I was in danger?" I ask, and she tenses before she looks at me fully.

"What do you mean in danger?" she asks.

"You know that the women all have gifts like we do. Well, I have been helping them because together, we can find other women who have gone missing and help heal certain people in the Elementals. What you don't know is that all the Elementals can bend an element, and they do this because they all are different like we are in a way." At Sara's confused look, I continue trying to explain without actually telling her that they aren't really human.

"They have many enemies because of the way they are. The Keres who were after us are their main threat. I didn't want you to think that I was in more danger because of this and try to get us out, because, Sara, I really love Caelius." As the words leave my mouth, I realise that I do love Caelius, and it's not a simple love. It's a deep, soul-shattering love that takes up my whole body, mind, and soul.

"I can see you love him, but I can also see that he loves you, and that is why I don't understand why you wouldn't tell me. I would never try to take you away from someone you care so much for."

I move over to the bench and sit down next to her. "I know that Joshua will still try to take us away if he thinks we are in danger, and I didn't want you to say anything to him that could lead him to do that."

She nods. "I know that you have been worried about Joshua, but so have I, and I would never do anything to harm him in any way. Contrary to what you might think, I'm not completely stupid, and I know that if he has to try to take us away again, the guys here will not take it lightly, especially not Caelius. Therefore, I would never do anything to hurt you or Joshua." I wish I could tell her the whole truth, but that I will leave to the men's discretion, as that is not something I can tell without them knowing.

"I love you, Sara, and you know I would never do anything purposefully to hurt you." At my words, she nods and then leans forward and hugs me. As her arms enfold me, I feel the knot in my stomach start to diminish until we hear a roar and then quiet.

"What the hell is going on?" she asks as she sits back.

"You know how I told you that the other women and I have been helping the Elementals with healing?" At Sara's nod, I continue. "Well, some of the guys don't want to wait, and they have come here insisting on being put at the top of the list. I think you can guess that the men here are not the type to be blackmailed."

"Are you saying that they are fighting?" Sara asks with a frightened look on her face.

"Yes, they are, but don't worry, they can take care of themselves." I see her face lose all colour. "What's wrong? Don't worry, nothing will happen to us. We are safe here," I insist, trying to calm the fear I can see.

"Is Gunner with them?" At her question, I realize that her fear is for Gunner and not so much for herself.

"Are you in love with Gunner?" She starts to shake her head but then stops and nods once.

"Oh, Sara." I pull her towards me again, hugging her close. "Don't worry, sweetheart, he will be fine."

"I'm being silly. It's not as if we are even together," she mumbles. "And he's so frustrating." At her grumbled reply, I smile in amusement.

"You want to tell me what's going on?"

She lifts her head and looks at me for a moment before she shrugs. "Gunner has kissed me a few times, but he's so frustrating," she mutters. "One minute he's hot, and then he's cold. I don't know what to think." I can see the frustration on her face. I figure that he's most probably like that because of what he is and doesn't know how to tell her. Caelius told me about how Gunner was at death's door and Brielle saved him by giving him Draco's blood, but in doing so, it changed him. He isn't an Elemental, but he isn't human either, and that might be why he is reluctant to be with Sara.

"Have you asked him about it?"

"No. What am I supposed to ask him?" she says as she lifts her hands in defeat.

"Don't ask him anything. Just tell him how you feel." At my answer, she looks at me with a surprised look.

"You think I should? What if this is just him playing around?" I shake my head at her insecurities; never have I seen Sara insecure before.

"Where has your courage gone? The Sara I know would go right up to him and tell him what she thinks."

She smiles at me and then nods. "You're right. I will go up to him and ask him what he wants." She stretches out and hugs me again. "Thank you, Sis," she murmurs, which warms my heart knowing that I was able to appease her.

CAELIUS 16

"Six of them, Draco. We killed six fucking Elementals," Burkhart grunts as he slaps the flat of his hand on the table. "Couldn't they see we were trying to help them? Damn selfish bastards." Burkhart has been raving ever since we got back into the compound. We are all upset with today's outcome. We knew that there might be brothers who would want preferential treatment or give us some trouble about it, but to blatantly challenge Draco, that is something new altogether.

Draco has been sitting back in his chair, watching everyone for the last ten minutes that we have been here; I know that his fury is being contained by his willpower alone. Having to kill those men today was torture for everyone, but for Draco, it's a betrayal of all the things he fought his whole life for.

"Burkhart, enough," I say, hoping that he finally settles down and lets us begin. He mutters but sits back in his chair, his arms crossed over his chest. The rest of us are all sitting in silence, each one in his own turmoil.

"We need to let Diesel know," Celmund suddenly states. This is going to be a blow for Diesel too, because those men have been with him for centuries like we have with Draco. "I can call him if you guys want."

"No," Draco states. His words are low and intense, the same as his eyes. We all know that he's struggling with his temper, and that just makes us respect him more. If it was anyone else, they would have succumbed to their inner turmoil long ago, but not Draco. This man before us will fight himself until he can't fight any longer before he will give in.

"Do you think there will be more?" Brandr asks as he rubs his forehead.

"I fucking hope not, because killing brothers is not cool," Ceric mutters.

"How many have been booked?" Wulf asks.

"We have one every day of the fucking week except for weekends as we agreed," Celmund states angrily. "The women are fully booked for the next eight weeks." From everyone, he is the one who has been dealing with the men as they try to get earlier bookings.

"What happens if we have an emergency? Do you think it will be a problem?"

Celmund shrugs. "I have thought about that, and the only way we're going to get away with slotting someone else in is if the women do the two in the same day." There are grunts around the table, as none of us want the women to do more than they should.

"This is becoming a fucking problem," Cassius mutters angrily. "We try to help these fuckers, and they give us grief."

"Do you need help?" I ask, looking at Celmund. It can't be easy for him having to deal with all the men and then still trying to find the mates of the men the women heal.

"It will become difficult to find these women if there is a new one every day." He looks at Draco and then back at us. "We need to see what we're going to do when we find the mates. Are we going to bring them here—"

"We don't bring anyone here," Draco interrupts. "You find them; give the brother the information, and he can go get his mate himself."

"What if they need more help? You know our women aren't like other women," Celmund says.

"They all belong to a chapter. The others there can help them," Draco states with a deadly look at Celmund that dares him to challenge his decision. Celmund lifts his hands in acquiescence, knowing that there is no use arguing with Draco when he has that tone of voice. "I want the gates closed; no one comes in without prior approval."

"Are we expecting problems?" Bjarni asks as he punches his fist into his hand.

"We always expect problems," Draco grunts.

"What do you want to do about what happened today?" Wulf asks as he sits forward. "There will be talk as soon as it is known that we killed six brothers."

"There is nothing to be done, is there?" Draco asks. "They attacked us, and we defended ourselves. If anyone has a problem with that, they can come talk to me." The meeting continues in the same kind of vein for the next hour until it finally draws to a close. As I'm about to walk out, I hear Draco tell Wulf that he's riding into town.

"I'll come with you." Draco looks over at me with a frown. "I need to go pick up Alaia's kutte anyway," I say before Draco can give me an excuse. I see Wulf's mouth kick up at the corner at my underhandedness.

"Fine, I'm leaving now." He makes his way towards me. When he's next to me, he stops. "Don't think I don't know what you're doing," he says with a raised brow before he walks out of the computer room. We are nearly by the garage when we see Celmund coming towards us from the bar.

"Where are you off to?"

"Town, and I guess you're coming too," Draco mutters as he continues to walk. I want to throw back my head and laugh at Draco's sarcastic reply. He knows that we will never let him go out on his own, like any other brother isn't allowed out on his own, even though he's more than capable of taking care of himself. Celmund looks at me and smirks as he shrugs, but he, too, walks with us to the garage.

"What is this, a fucking intervention?" I hear Draco mutter as we reach the garage. I look around him and can't help myself as I throw back my head and roar with laughter when I see Brandr and Ceric already sitting on their bikes, waiting for us.

Draco looks back at me and raises his brow. "I don't see how this is amusing, asshole." But there is a twitch to his lips as he walks towards his bike. "Seeing you all tagging along, who's paying for the drinks?" he asks as he sits on his bike.

"I'll pay first round," Ceric offers with a grin as he starts his bike.

"Well, then, what are we waiting for?" Draco asks as he accelerates and is out of the garage and towards the main gate. Draco takes the lead as we ride towards town, but just before town, Draco turns into a pub we haven't frequented in a while. Before the men started to meet their mates, we used to come here often, as we didn't really cook much, and our meals were taken wherever we could find them.

We used to have Jezebels at the compound, but they weren't much good at cooking as they were at other things. After we started to find that the mates didn't like the idea of the Jezebels around, we got rid of them to other chapters. In all the years that we have lived together, never have I seen the men as content as they are now. It is amazing how at peace and content we feel just because we have found someone who understands us, who we can open up fully and talk to with no thought of being judged.

When there is unconditional love, nothing else can compare. I feel Alaia's vulnerability sometimes when she speaks of things, but she has realized that nothing she can tell me will change the way I see her or think of her.

"Are you coming?" Brandr asks as the guys start making their way inside and I am still sitting on my bike.

"Yeah," I grunt as I dismount and make my way after them. When we walk in, the smell of food and drink accosts me, also the noise of the rowdy clientele who usually frequent the pub.

"I can't believe it," Suzy says as she sees us. Suzy is one of the waitresses who has been working at the pub for as long as it has been open. She's a bit of a tease and always happy to lay with the guys, but a good woman in general. She rushes up to Draco, who is the first one in the door, and hugs him before kissing his cheek. "I thought we had done something wrong. None of you ever came back in here." She moves towards Ceric, but he quickly rushes towards an empty table, which makes me grin, until I see her coming my way.

Fuck, the last thing I want is for her to kiss me. The thought of her touching me has my skin crawling. The guys weren't joking when they said that we have a repelling effect when women touch us. "Caelius, I've missed you," she says as she hugs me.

"Hi, Suzy," I mutter. "How have you been?"

"Okay, but I'm much better now that I have you guys here." I give her a smile but also make my way towards the table Ceric arranged for us.

"Chicken," I mutter as I sit before him, and he shrugs.

"Rather be chicken than have that creepy feeling running over my skin," he says with a grin. "I'm feeling fine now, and you are trying to get rid of that feeling of having cheated on your woman." I'm about to answer when I shut my mouth and realize that what he is saying is true. There is a feeling as if I did something I wasn't supposed to do, a feeling of having cheated on my woman. I shake my head.

"This really sucks," I mutter, and he laughs as Brandr and Celmund sit down as Draco drags a chair from another table towards ours.

"What sucks?" Celmund asks as he looks around. As Elementals, we are always prepared. As soon as we enter a place, we make sure we know who and what is around us.

"He just had his first encounter with a woman since bonding," Ceric quips, which has Brandr and Celmund grinning.

"You have all turned soft," Draco quips as he smiles at Suzy as she approaches. I can see by the charm he is exuding that she will be spending the night with him tonight; maybe we should have left him to his own devices today. After Suzy takes our orders, I sit back and look around at the other clients.

I notice a table with five men sitting at a corner table. My instincts tell me that they are not regular customers. Their shoes are way too clean for this area, and their clothes clearly state that they are carrying weapons. I'm about to mention it to the others, when Draco catches my eye and shakes his head, letting me know he has seen them.

"Ceric, what are you going to do now that you're going to become a dad?" Celmund asks with a twinkle in his eye.

"What do you mean? Do about what?" Ceric asks with a frown.

"Well, you don't want your kid to see that your woman beats you, do you?" Celmund teases, which has us all grinning. We usually tease Ceric about Nova because of her being such a spitfire, but she's a good woman and he's lucky to have her. He shows Celmund the finger with a grin of his own.

"You wish your woman had the fire mine has," he teases as he winks.

"No, it's fine; at least I'll still have hair, as yours seems to be receding with the heat." We all laugh at that, as Ceric had to cut his hair shorter a few days ago because of one of Burkhart's fire-bending experiments, which he was not impressed about.

"Yeah, yeah, very funny," he mutters as he rubs his shorter hair. "Nova was not impressed."

"I noticed. Even Burkhart stayed out of her way that day," Brandr says with a laugh.

"Yeah, she hasn't got much patience lately," Ceric says, "but I have found a way to calm her."

"We have noticed with the boxes of marshmallows arriving every day at the compound," Draco mutters.

"What?" Ceric says as he raises his arms in defeat. "Bion said that we must give pregnant women whatever they want."

"Yes, in moderation, dude," Brandr grunts. "You bought a whole truck. Everyone is eating marshmallows to try to finish them."

"Well, then, you should say thank you," Ceric quips. "You're the one with the sweet tooth. I'm sure you have a packet in your pocket right now."

"Nope. If I don't see a marshmallow in the next century, it will be too soon," Brandr grunts with a grimace.

"Here you go," Suzy says as she places our drinks on the table, and then she leans over Draco's shoulder and kisses his neck, but before standing again, she whispers in his ear. I see Draco tense, and then his hand lifts and pulls her down again, and he takes her lips in a blistering kiss.

"Thanks," he grunts as he lets her go. As she starts to walk away, we all look at him, waiting for him to tell us what has placed him on alert.

"The group of guys in the far corner are very interested in us. Apparently they just had one of the guys place a tracker on one of our bikes." At his words, Celmund pulls out his phone and starts to text.

"Sons of bitches. Who the fuck are they now?" Ceric mutters angrily.

"Caelius, you're in the right angle to take photos of them. I'm not. Try to get a picture of each one of them." At Celmund's request, I take out my phone, making as if I'm texting, and start to take photos. When I'm sure I have one of each of them, I send them to him.

"Cassius will see if they pop up in the system. In the meantime, I think we should start heading back. I will scan the bikes when we get outside and see which one has the tracker." We quickly finish our drinks and then make our way outside. Celmund stops by each of the bikes, talking to each one of us as he scans the bikes, making so that if anyone is watching, they won't know that we have realized what they have done.

"Guess who the lucky winner is," he says as he sits on his bike and stretches forward to start it. "Me." He grins as he shakes his head. I smile, as I can image how he's going to scramble that tracker to lead them to somewhere else. We all head back to the compound to go figure out who those assholes who were so curious about us are.

ALAIA 17

"Are you all ready for him?" Bion asks as he walks into the room next to where the man we are going to help today is waiting. We had someone this morning, but this guy came in as an emergency. Apparently his rages are getting out of control. Bion walks towards Brielle and hugs her close, kissing her forehead.

"I think so," I murmur as I lean back against Caelius. To be honest, I'm slightly tired from the previous healing, but I won't confess, or the men won't let us continue. I also know that the man we are about to heal will drain us, as his energy is peaking with fury. I know Brielle is feeling as drained as I am, which will make the healing more complicated, but we will manage.

"Well, then, it's time to start, as I don't think he can hold on much longer. You sure you're okay to do this?" he asks Brielle, which has her smiling at him and nodding.

"I'm fine, don't worry." She lifts onto her toes and kisses him lightly on the lips before moving away towards where we usually sit to start the treatments. Caelius lowers his head and kisses my neck before stepping back; he turns me around in his arms until I'm facing him.

"If it looks like he's draining you, I'm stopping this," he mutters with a frown.

"You know you can't interrupt a treatment. Don't worry, the other women are supporting us with their energy." I try to appease with my words even though I know that the others are just as tired as me from having these treatments every day. He lifts his hand and strokes my cheek gently before nodding even though I can see that my words have done nothing to quieten his worry. He turns and leaves. I know that he will be in the computer room with some of the other men.

I walk towards where I usually sit, and groan as I touch the ground and feel the anger vibrating through it. "This one is going to be hectic. His energy is vibrating through the ground," I warn everyone as I wait for them to take their places.

Closing my eyes, I feel the other women's energy start to flow through me. I relax my body and then connect to my surroundings, feeling the vibrations of the earth around me. I find the connection with the man and start by sending our energy through to him. As soon as our soothing energy touches his soul, there is an explosive thrust of anger rushing towards us. I hear murmurs of pain as the others feel his energy.

I call for help from Mother Nature, who surrounds us to help soothe this man's fury, help calm his rage, and once again send another vibration of love towards him. Once again, his energy attacks us with a burst of its own negative energy. I hear someone gasp behind me in pain, and then the link with all the women is broken. I can feel myself tumbling through a void as I try to pull myself away from this negative energy that surrounds me.

When I finally open my eyes, I hear laboured breathing. Looking around, I see Jasmine lying on the floor as if passed out, Aria is gasping for air, Brielle still has her eyes closed and is as white as a sheet, and then I hear a whimper. Looking back, I see Nova hunched forward, holding her belly.

"Nova?" My voice is raspy from the energy I can still feel coursing through my body.

"Something is wrong," she murmurs. She doesn't open her eyes but continues to hold her stomach as if in pain.

My head is spinning as I try to move. It feels like my muscles won't cooperate, and then I hear a roar, and the door to where we are snaps back and hits the wall as Ceric rushes in.

"Hellcat?" he says as he kneels next to Nova, but still, she doesn't open her eyes, but I see tears coursing down her cheeks. "What's wrong? Talk to me," he mumbles as he pulls her into his arms, and then she cries out in pain, which has him freezing, all colour leaving his face.

I'm seeing everything as if from afar. Wulf is picking up Jasmine, trying to awaken her, but she's lying limply in his arms. Bion is talking to Brielle, but she still has her eyes closed. Caelius has his arms around me and is talking to me, but I can't hear what he's saying as my mind starts to spin. I try to focus. I need to know what is happening and how the others are doing, but my mind doesn't want to cooperate.

And then I feel the tremors start deep within me, and my body starts to shake. "Fuck, Bion, what the hell is happening to her?" I hear Caelius shout, and even though I want to calm him, I can't stop the tremors. I feel Caelius's lips close to my forehead as he murmurs to me, but I can't tell what he's saying, and then everything darkens, and I feel myself lose consciousness.

I don't know how long I'm out for, but suddenly, there is a roar that has my heart pounding. I try to open my eyes, but they're still not cooperating with me. "Hold him the fuck down," I hear Burkhart mutter. I wonder what's wrong. Who is losing control that they have to hold him down? Maybe the guy we are supposed to help finally lost his fight and is turning Keres.

"What do you think I'm doing?" Celmund grunts.

"Calm down or I'm going to knock you out. Think of your woman. This isn't helping her." At those words, I hear a scuffle and then another roar.

"I'm going to kill that son of a bitch." That is Ceric. Then everything comes back to me, and I remember that Nova was in pain. Did something happen to Nova? To the baby? My eyes slit open, and I realize I'm in the infirmary. Burkhart and Celmund are holding Ceric down while Caelius and Draco have Wulf against the wall. I turn my head and see Bion standing over Nova as he monitors her vitals.

Jasmine is in the bed opposite her. I see a pale Saskia and Talia standing near her bed. "Are you okay?" I look down and see that Brielle is sitting on a chair next to me. If I have to guess, I think she looks as bad as I do. I think we are both drained. I don't know what happened, but whatever it was, it knocked us all out.

"Just tired," I murmur.

"Kitten." I turn my head at Caelius's call and see him looking over his shoulder. "Are you okay?" I can see the strain on his face as he exerts himself to hold on to a furious Wulf.

"Yes." My voice comes out in a rasp, but I know that he heard me, as he closes his eyes before turning his head again to look at Wulf.

"Shit," Bion suddenly mutters, which has me looking at him. He's looking over at Ceric, who has a scowl on his face. "Ceric, your woman needs you. Fuck . . ." He places his hand over her stomach.

"Do you need me?" Brielle asks as she tries to stand from the chair.

"Stay there. You're in no condition to help, and I can't worry about you now, beauty," he mutters as he rushes to get a tray with medical equipment on it.

"Hellcat," Ceric roars from where he's face down with Burkhart holding his arms behind him.

"If you want to go to your woman, calm the fuck down," Burkhart says angrily as he pulls at his arms.

"Ceric, she needs you now," Bion roars. I look back at Bion and see him holding a scalpel. I feel my stomach turn at the thought of him cutting into Nova. I quickly turn my head again and see Celmund and Burkhart lifting Ceric off the floor and dragging him towards where Bion and Nova are. I hear Ceric's roar of pain, but I don't look, as I can feel the tears filling my eyes.

I hope the baby is okay, and Nova has to be fine, because things won't be the same without her. Looking at Caelius, I see Wulf falling forward and Draco helping him to the floor. Caelius shakes his head and then says something to Draco before he turns and walks towards me. When he's standing next to the bed, I can see the lines of stress on his face. "I don't want you to do that again," he mutters as he strokes the hair away from my face.

"I'm okay," I say, but he shakes his head, a frown appearing on his face.

"No, you're not okay. None of you are okay," he grunts. His hand goes up and pulls his fingers through his hair. He looks towards where Bion and the others are, and I see a concerned look on his face.

"What happened?" he asks as he looks back at me.

I shrug as I think back to what happened. "We were healing him the same way we always do, when he used the same method to send a flash of rage our way." I think of the impact of that rage, of how it filled my senses and how it must have reached the other women too. "I think one of us must have cut the connection when that happened." That is the only explanation I can think of. If the connection was cut between our energy, then it might affect us this way, as we didn't have time to centre our energy again.

"Are you in any pain, kitten?" His hand is moving over my body to make sure I'm still in one piece, his eyes following his hand.

"Yes, I'm fine. Just still a bit dizzy. I just need to rest a bit and I will be fine," I promise just as we hear Ceric muttering. The worry is stronger than me, so I turn my head to look to see what is happening. At first, I can't see anything, as Burkhart and Celmund are standing in the way, but then Celmund moves slightly, and I can see Ceric hunched over Nova, his head next to hers as he talks to her even though I see that she's unconscious.

I can't see what's happening with the men standing before me, but I know that Bion is working on Nova by the sounds coming from the other bed. "Bring me the incubator," I hear Bion say suddenly, and then there is a rush of activity.

"Come, kitten; let me take you to our room so they have more space in here and so you can relax," Caelius says as he picks me up against his chest. He kisses my forehead as he turns to walk out. "Let me know what's happening," I hear him say to someone as we walk out. I know that today was a step back from everything we have been trying to do, but it's only with the mistakes that sometimes we can better things. Therefore, I'm hoping this will make us stronger and more capable of helping. I'm also praying that this setback doesn't hurt us in a way we will never recover from.

"How is Jasmine?" I ask as Caelius enters our room and places me on our bed.

"I'm not sure; Bion hasn't had a chance to look at her, as Nova needed his help. That's why Wulf was losing his shit." I can hear the concern in his voice. "This can't happen again, kitten; you women are the most important part of our existence. We will not have any of you in danger or hurt again."

"This is just a setback. Once we figure out what happened, we can prevent it," I state as I feel my eyes closing once again in exhaustion.

"Good luck convincing us, because I can tell you now I for one don't want you to do that again," Caelius mutters. I want to argue with him so he can realize that what happened today doesn't necessarily mean that it will happen again, but sleep pulls me under.

CAELIUS 18

I pull at my hair in frustration; we have been going around and around with this meeting, and it's getting us nowhere. It has been a week since the incident, and we now have the men who were booked complaining, and even though the women have insisted on continuing with the healing, we will not approve it. Ceric and Nova's baby is still struggling to survive, Nova nearly died, and Jasmine took two days before she woke up.

"Is it possible that was the reason for what happened?" Draco asks again as Celmund plays the video of what happened on the day of the incident.

"The women seem to think it is, and I think that according to the way their energy works, it is possible that when Nova pulled back and broke the connection with all of them, they didn't have time to rein in their energy, and that is the reason for what happened." I know what Celmund is explaining, as Alaia has been saying the same thing for the last few days, but that doesn't calm my mind or any of the others' minds either.

"Is there any way of stopping that from happening again?" Draco asks.

"Fuck, Draco," Brandr mutters as he throws up his hands.

"No fucking way," Cassius grunts as he stands.

"I want to have all the details, because we have the women insisting on continuing, and we have the brothers up in arms because now they want the treatments. I know you want to protect your women. I fucking want them safe too, but for that, we need to make sure that we know everything we can, because you all know that they will go ahead sooner or later and try to heal even without our permission." At Draco's words, I tense, knowing that what he says is true. I have asked Alaia not to tire herself out, as I can clearly see that she's still tired even after resting for the last week.

She has been staying in bed, but I think that's because she hasn't the strength to get up, but I know that as soon as she's able, she will want to continue, because as she says, this is their calling, and we can't stop them from helping if that is what they want to do.

"That's not going to happen, Draco. Jasmine's not going to be doing this again," Wulf states angrily.

"How many times have you tried to stop her, Brother? It has never worked before. Do you think it will stop her now?" What Draco says is true. Wulf has tried to stop Jasmine from using her gift many times, as he didn't want her being hurt in any way, but every time, she has gone against his wishes and used them again, and usually to our benefit.

"Nova nearly died, Jasmine was out for three days, and the others are still trying to recuperate," Wulf growls. "How the fuck can they want to carry on with this?"

"They say it's their calling," I mutter.

"Well, they can fucking change that calling," Bjarni states as he bangs his hand on the table.

"You all know as well as me that they are not going to stop just because you tell them to. Isn't it better to try to prevent another incident like what happened?" Draco asks as he leans back in his chair. "I gave them my word that they could help us. I can't go back on that. If you can convince them to stop using their gifts, then so be it, but if you aren't able, then I can't stop them either."

I know what he says is true, but that doesn't make it better, because I know that Alaia is going to try to help as soon as she's able.

"What if we get some kind of ties that will tie them to the woman they are supposed to be touching until they're ready to let go?" Bion suggests, which has the men glaring at him. "What? Do you think I want Brielle to use her gift again? Well, I don't, but as it has been stated here, that is part of who she is, and I won't ever be able to stop her, so I might as well try to figure out the best way to help her."

"What kind of ties were you thinking about?" I ask, and Burkhart shakes his head in anger.

"I was thinking something leather that would hold the one's wrist to the other one's arm or leg," Bion says.

"I've seen something like that," Gunner says. "You might have to adjust it, but the ones that are used in sexual play to tie a person down can work." At Gunner's response, we all look at him with raised brows. Well, guess we know what he's into.

"You don't perhaps have one lying around, do you?" Celmund teases.

"Wouldn't you like to know?" he jokes with a wink. "But I'm sure I can find a place that would have them." After that, the meeting centres on how we're going to protect our women from getting hurt and not so much on how to stop them. We all agree that we will try to stop them, but we are also all fairly certain that we won't be able to get that right.

"I've stopped the bookings until we see what is happening, and have contacted the ones who are scheduled for them to know that there might be a delay," Celmund informs everyone.

"What happened with Diesel? How did he take the news that his men turned on us?" I ask. It has been so hectic these last few days that I had completely forgotten about the brothers we killed.

"He didn't take it well, but he understood. He will let me know how the others take it. Also, I have informed the other chapters and am awaiting a reaction from them," Draco updates with a shrug.

"We have another problem," Celmund says. "The guys who placed the tracker on my bike belong to a private organization." I had forgotten about those fuckers. Why would a private organization be interested in bikers? The thought has chills rising over my skin as I think of the assholes who grabbed me before. I know it can't be them because we eradicated the whole group who thought to hurt me.

"What private organization?" Burkhart asks as he sits forward with his elbows on the table.

"One that has mercenaries working for them, and for some reason, they have been sniffing around, trying to get information about us." That is all we need right now, another complication.

"Do you know why?" Wulf asks with a frown.

"The only thing I found that would link them to us is that Alaia and Sara's brother works for them." At my woman's name, I tense. Is her fucking brother trying to cause problems?

"What does he do there?" I ask with a frown.

"He's one of the mercenaries, but he wasn't one of the guys we took photos of at that table." At Celmund's comment, I shake my head in confirmation. "They have been looking into the club, which I'm guessing is on their brother's behalf."

"Should I speak to him?" I ask, and look over at Draco, who is frowning.

"I think he's worried about his sisters' welfare. Has he been speaking to them?" Draco asks.

"He won't answer their calls. Alaia tried, but he's rejected every call," I state in anger. I have asked Alaia if she would like me to have a word with him, but she insists that she doesn't. I know that her brother ignoring her is hurting her deeply, but there is nothing I can do if she doesn't want me to get involved, but if he is digging into club business, that is something completely different.

"They won't find anything," Celmund promises. "I don't think it's necessary that you talk to him unless you want to, or unless he starts to become a problem." I know that no one will be able to find any trail regarding our connection to the Bratva Mafia and the agreement we have. There is also nothing that they could possibly find regarding us being Elementals, as Celmund has made sure to keep us off social media and any other platform that could reveal us.

"What does this organization do that they need paid mercenaries?" Bion asks with a frown.

"They're into armament," Celmund reveals. "But nothing like what we transport for Alexey." Draco has an agreement with Alexey, the Bratva Mafia boss. We transport all their guns up into Africa for them, and they help us when we need eyes and help in finding the women the Keres kidnap.

"You don't think it could have something to do with that?" Burkhart asks.

"No. Compared to this organization, Alexey is small fry. They supply the army and navy. They won't be worried about the weapons we transport."

"Well, then, I guess we will just have to keep an eye on them and maybe try to get the women to contact him again and try to appease his worry," Draco states as he looks at me and then at Gunner.

"What?" Gunner asks as he sees the look, and then Draco lifts his eyebrow in amusement. We have all seen the looks flying between Gunner and Sara. "I will talk to her."

"That should go well," Cassius quips, "going by the glare I saw her throwing your way this morning." We all grin when Gunner shows him the finger.

"Well, if there is nothing else, you can leave," Draco states as he leans back in his chair. "Bion, I need to talk to you." I can see the stress on his face, and I know he wants to know about how Nova and Jasmine are doing and how Ceric is hanging in there. Since the incident, Ceric has been sitting in the infirmary with his woman and their son. He will only leave to shower, and then he's back. The women have been taking him food, and we have taken turns sitting with him when Nova is sleeping. We know that this has shaken him up. Ceric isn't the type to show his emotions, and it affects him deeply when people are hurting.

I leave the two to their conversation and walk out; I'm about to head towards the room, when I sense that Alaia is in the kitchen. What the hell is she doing up and about already? Looking inside, I see her sitting with Sara and Brielle. When she sees me, a guilty look appears on her face, and then she smiles—a naughty smile that instantly has my cock reacting. I decide not to say anything. If she feels like she's better to be up and about, then I will leave her to it.

"It's good that the two of you are together," I say as I walk in. I lean down and kiss Alaia on the lips before taking the chair next to hers. "Hi, Brielle. You're looking well rested," I tease, as I know that Bion has been insisting on her resting every day for a couple hours, which she is starting to rebel against.

"Don't get me started," she teases as she sticks out her tongue at me playfully.

"So why are you happy that we're together?" Sara asks with a raised brow as she takes a sip of her coffee. I've noticed that Sara isn't the type to mince words. She says what she thinks when she thinks it, which is refreshing. Not always for Gunner, but I think he's enjoying it.

"Joshua is snooping into our things. Is there any way you two can get him to talk to you and realize that we're not hurting you in any way?" At my question, I see both of them tense and then look at each other.

"Should we?" Alaia asks, which has Sara smiling widely.

"I think we should. It has always worked before," Sara replies with a laugh.

"He is going to be so angry," Alaia states with a grin, which has me thinking that whatever they're planning can't be too bad if it has both of them smiling.

"What are both of you up to?" I ask suspiciously. I will not let them leave and then get picked up by Joshua, where he will not let them return. Not that it would stop me, because now that we are bonded, I will find my woman anywhere and bring her back to me. Thinking about that, I have something I need to give her.

"When we were younger and Joshua didn't let us tag along or when he was angry with us, I would hold him down and Sara and I would nag him until he gave in," Alaia confesses with a blush on her face.

"How did you hold him down, kitten? He was already older than you, and I'm sure you two were tiny little wisps," I ask with amusement, as I can imagine these two ganging up against their brother.

"Once I got roots from the trees to hold him down. Another time, his ankles sank into the earth and held him tight." I throw back my head and laugh in amusement at what these two have gotten up to.

"I want to see you laugh when she does that to you," Sara teases, which instantly has my cock twitching again.

"If she holds me down and has her way with me, she can do it anytime she wants," I tease, which makes Alaia's cheeks burst with colour, but a naughty look enters her eyes. Brielle and Sara burst out laughing.

"Ew, too much information," Sara jokes as Alaia leans forward and kisses my lips and then moves back slightly and winks.

"That could be arranged," she whispers, which has me wanting to pick her up and rush to our room.

"Okay, you two, we are sitting right here," Brielle teases, which unfortunately has Alaia moving back as she winks at me naughtily.

"Sara will find him, and then we will have to get closer to him, but once we're close enough, I can hold him down, and we can both go convince the stubborn ass," Alaia says, which has me tensing.

"You have to leave the compound?" I don't like that idea at all.

"Unless he's here, how else are we supposed to talk to him?" Sara asks with a questioning look.

"I don't like the idea of you two being outside," I state. "Sara, if you find him, I will organize the brothers, and we will accompany you."

"I'm sure that won't be necessary," Alaia says.

"That's the only way I'm letting you out of here. I'm not going to let you be outside in danger," I state. Alaia frowns and then looks at Sara, who shrugs. She then looks at me and nods.

ALAIA 19

I can see Joshua from where we stopped. Sara found him, but at the time, he was with two other men. We made our way to this field where men were training. The men parked their bikes a few metres away as not to be seen or heard, and then accompanied us here. We are standing unseen at the moment, waiting for Joshua to be by himself before I can do anything. Caelius is standing behind me, his arms around my waist as he looks around, making sure everything is safe.

I notice Gunner standing next to Sara even though she's been glaring at him as often as possible. Celmund, Bion, and Burkhart are in different locations, and Cassius stayed by the bikes in case someone found them.

"Looks like they're finally leaving," Sara murmurs. "Maybe do it before he gets into his car." I look over at Joshua's SUV and nod. It would be the perfect place, as his SUV is close to the trees and covers anyone by the building from seeing us talking to him.

When we finally see Joshua walking towards his car, I kneel to the ground and touch the earth. Closing my eyes, I connect with Mother Earth and ask for her assistance. When Joshua reaches for his door handle, roots shoot up from the ground and circle his feet and lower legs. He looks down and then tries to rip them apart with his hands. Shoots shoot up from the ground and circle his wrists, stopping him from moving.

"Alaia!" he roars. I stand from where I'm kneeling and start to walk forward, but Caelius places a hand on my upper arm and stops me. He looks to his left at Celmund, who is closer to the building. I see Celmund nod, and then he guides me forward.

"It will be better if I go alone with Sara," I state, as I know Joshua will take it easier if we're alone.

"I'm not leaving you in the open alone," he mutters as he continues to walk forward.

"Listen to me." I stop, not taking another step. "If you want this to work, you have to let me do this. You can protect me from somewhere hidden." I can see the fight going on in his head, but I won't move if he insists on this, because I know Joshua. He will never give in if he knows the men are close.

"Okay, but if I tell you something, do it straight away. Don't ask questions," he says. I nod and then kiss him quickly before making my way towards Joshua, Sara right next to me. Caelius and Gunner move towards the trees and follow us from their cover.

"Joshua," I say, walking around so I can see his face, as he was half turned towards the car.

"Alaia, let me go. We're not kids anymore," he mutters.

"Oh, well, you were acting like one, so I'm treating you like one," I mutter. "Why weren't you answering any of our calls?"

"Because the two of you weren't being rational," he mutters as he glares at us.

"Why? Because we didn't do what you wanted us to do?" Sara asks. "We are grownups, Joshua. We have a right to choose what we want to do with our lives."

"They are bikers. You don't know what bikers are like," he argues.

"Those bikers and their wives have treated us better than most people we meet," I say with a frown. "Don't judge people just because of appearances. You better than anyone should know that." Joshua knows how Sara and I struggled with our gifts, with hiding it from everyone, especially when we were small. He was always the one to fight others when they called us freaks when we were small, and now he is judging people he doesn't even know.

"Josh, I know you're only thinking of our welfare, but we are honestly happy, and they are really good to us," Sara says as she moves closer to him.

"You were there less than a day and already sleeping with them," he mutters. "I don't want you mixed up with the wrong people. You two are still too sheltered; you don't know how people can be." He tries to loosen his hands again. I step closer and take his hand in mine.

"Joshua, you know us. Look at the two of us. Do we look like we aren't happy? Do we look as if we are doing anything we don't want to do?" I ask, and can feel his anger dispersing as he looks at us.

"Yes, they're bikers, but they also like everyone else, and they are really kind to us," Sara says.

"Do they know about your gifts?" he asks.

"Yes, they do, and they don't care," I say, not elaborating on the others at the compound.

"Why would you tell about your gift when you never tell anyone?" Joshua asks suspiciously.

"One of the women there has a gift like ours, and they accept her fully," Sara says suddenly, which has me breathing out in relief, as I don't like lying to anyone. I see Joshua analysing us as if he can tell the truth just by looking at us, and I know he's still worried but will trust us with this.

"I had some people look into them, and up to now, we haven't been able to find anything," he says suddenly. "Are you sure you are happy there and that everything is going fine?" Both of us nod at the same time. I let go of his hand and stretch up to kiss his cheek, and Sara does the same.

"Because I know that you will try to retaliate, I'm going to leave, and when I'm a fair distance away, I will let you go," I say with a smile, and see his grin, because when I was young, I learnt my lesson with him. "And from now on, answer our calls, or next time, it will be worse." I turn and make my way back to where the bikes are.

When I can see Caelius and Gunner by the trees, I lean down and ask that Joshua be set free, not looking back as I make my way towards my future. Caelius opens his arms as I approach, and I slide my arms around his waist as his arms come around me. "Let's go home," I say, and Caelius nods before he lets go and guides me towards the bikes.

I see that Gunner is walking behind Sara, his eyes roving over the terrain, making sure there is no threat to us. I am still wondering how I was so lucky to have found a man like Caelius, and how out of everyone in this universe, I am the woman meant for him. He helps me onto the bike, and a few minutes later, we are riding home, the wind surrounding us with its touch.

When we arrive, instead of going into the compound, Caelius asks if I would like to go for a walk, as he wants to talk to me. I look into his face and realize that he looks nervous, something I have never seen him be before.

"What's wrong?" I ask, and he shrugs.

"Nothing. I just want alone time with you with no one around," he says as we start to walk on the path that leads to the lake. His arm surrounds my shoulders. As he hugs me close, his lips touch my forehead. "Are you more at peace now that your brother is convinced we aren't hurting you?"

"The three of us have always been close, so yes, it wasn't sitting well with me that he wasn't talking to me. I know he was worried about me and Sara, and I know that he was hurt because I chose to stay here instead of going with him." I try to explain to him how I felt and what this means to me. "Now that he's at peace with us staying here, I'm at peace."

Caelius doesn't say anything as we continue to walk down the path. When we reach the lake, we stop. As always, this place brings such peace, such contentment, that I could sit here for hours. "Let's sit over here,"

Caelius says as he guides me towards a large boulder near the water.

"You know, when I was young, I used to practice my bending near a lake very similar to this one," he says suddenly. "I would like you to meet my parents." At his words, I tense. Because of their age, I never thought about his parents, but of course he has parents.

"Where are they?" I ask. I can feel myself getting nervous, as I never thought I would get to meet his parents.

"They're not far. They live in a little town a few kilometres from here. I've told them about you, and I would like you to meet my sister." He has a sister? Now not only do I have to meet parents I had never thought about, but I also have a sister to impress.

"Do you think they're going to like me?" I ask.

"Don't frown, kitten. They will love you," he says with a smile as his thumb moves over my forehead to clear away my frown. "The same way as I love you." At his words, I freeze. I know he cares deeply for me, but he never said he loved me before. I can feel my heart start to race, and tears fill my eyes. I have quietly wished for these very words, scared that he wanted me simply for the reason that I'm his mate but not really loving me as a person.

To know that his heart beats for me has a tear slipping down my cheek. "I love you too, more than I ever thought I could love someone," I state as I lean forward and kiss his lips.

"Your love has healed me; the tear I felt in my soul is no longer bleeding with pain. Since my capture, a part of myself was lost, the joy ripped away from me." He strokes his finger over my cheek, cleaning away the tears. "My body was tortured and marked, and I thought that if I did find my mate one day, it would be wrong of me to take her and have her accept someone who had been touched by so much evil, who wasn't perfect for her." He takes in a deep breath and then looks towards the water.

"But when I met you, I couldn't let you go. I couldn't see myself living the rest of my empty existence without you. Your touch calms my soul, fills me with joy, something I haven't had in a very long time."

I had never thought that I would hear someone say these things to me; I have always been suspicious of love. For me, people love, but that changes with time. They say things on one day, and then the other, you find them doing something else that shows that what they said isn't what touched you the day before. But with Caelius, since the beginning, he has shown me how much he loves me. He has been gentle, caring, and so protective.

With Caelius, I feel his love. He hadn't given me the words, but he was giving me the actions every day. I never thought I would find this type of all-consuming love, a love that not only I feel but the other person shows me that he feels too.

Caelius pulls a small black cloth bag out of his jeans pocket, which has me frowning, as I can see that he is nervous. If he were human, I would think he was about to propose, but I know that Elementals don't consider marriage necessary, as their bond is unbreakable. I'm so curious that I want to snatch the bag away from him and peep inside. He opens the bag and pulls out a beautiful silver chain, and at the end of the chain is a beautiful lapis lazuli, similar to the one he always wears.

He opens the clasp and slides the chain around my neck. "I give you a part of my essence to protect and enhance your energy. By wearing this Lapis Lazuli, you will always have a piece of me with you. You are now part of my blood, my soul, my very essence. I ask that you wear this always to remind you of our bond and the love I hold for you." I am now crying openly, as I know that to the Elementals, this is an important part of their mating ritual.

These stones are forged for each one of them when they are born. They have their essence, and their mate is presented with their stone when she is ready to follow her mate through his eternal life and when he feels she has accepted him completely, as the stone is only wearable if the mate is completely one with her man.

"Thank you, my love. I will hold this stone close to my heart for all time. I never thought I would find someone like you. Someone who loves me openly and completely. I will always dedicate my love and my caring for you . . ."

"And any kids we may have," he says with a wink, which has my cheeks warming with embarrassment. We have never spoken about children, but I want to have them with Caelius. I can just imagine a little boy like him running around, a little boy who will grow up to be proud of the work his father does for his people, and that his mother and the women in the compound do for the other Elementals, because we will carry on healing, and hopefully the Keres will one day come to an end. We were told that as soon as we are all feeling up to it, we can continue with our work, if that is what we want.

"Yes, and any children we may have. Thank you, Caelius, for showing me this life and for filling my heart with so much love that sometimes it pains." Caelius lowers his head and takes my lips in a gentle kiss that binds our oaths together for all time.

THE END.

ABOUT THE AUTHOR

Alexi Ferreira, loves the idea of Alpha Men who take charge are possessive and care for their woman. She creates books that take you on an emotional journey whether tears, laughter or just steamy hotness. She loves to connect with readers and interacting with them through social media or even old fashioned email.

She currently lives in Johannesburg, South Africa.

Other books in the Elemental's MC:

- Wulf (Book 1)
- Bjarni (Book 2)
- Brandr (Book 3)
- Ceric (Book 4)
- Bion (Book 5)
- Cassius (Book 6)
- Celmund (Book 7)
- Burkhart (Book 8)
- Caelius (Book 9)
- Draco Salvation (Book 10)
- Draco Wrath (Book 11)

Join her newsletter to stay up to date as well as take part in giveaways and just let her know how you feel about her books!

Link: https://www.alexiferreira.writer.com/subscribe